14.45

MONET'S GHOST

Books from Byron Preiss Visual Publications and
Atheneum Books for Young Readers:

LETTERS FROM ATLANTIS
by Robert Silverberg

THE DREAMING PLACE
by Charles de Lint

THE SLEEP OF STONE
by Louise Cooper

BLACK UNICORN
by Tanith Lee

CHILD OF AN ANCIENT CITY
*by Tad Williams and
Nina Kiriki Hoffman*

DRAGON'S PLUNDER
by Brad Strickland

WISHING SEASON
by Esther M. Friesner

THE WIZARD'S APPRENTICE
by S. P. Somtow

GOLD UNICORN
by Tanith Lee

BORN OF ELVEN BLOOD
*by Kevin J. Anderson and
John Gregory Betancourt*

THE MONSTER'S LEGACY
by Andre Norton

THE ORPHAN'S TENT
by Tom De Haven

MONET'S GHOST
by Chelsea Quinn Yarbro

MONET'S GHOST

by
CHELSEA QUINN YARBRO

Illustrated by Pat Morrissey

A Byron Preiss Book

Atheneum Books for Young Readers

MONET'S GHOST
Dragonflight Books

Atheneum Books for Young Readers
An imprint of Simon & Schuster Children's Publishing Division
1230 Avenue of the Americas
New York, NY 10020

Cover painting by Pat Morrissey. Cover design by Brad Foltz
Edited by Keith R. A. DeCandido

Special thanks to Jonathan Lanman, Howard Kaplan, and
John Betancourt.

First Edition
Printed in the United States of America
10 9 8 7 6 5 4 3 2 1

ISBN 0-689-80732-5

Library of Congress Catalog Card Number: 96-85373

for
my cousin
Carol Hanni
who is something of an artist
herself
—C.Q.Y.

Prologue

When it happened the first time, Geena Howe was looking at a Mondrian canvas in the modern wing of the art museum, a painting her art teacher said was like a bad design for linoleum tile. But it didn't seem like that at all to Geena. The more she studied it, the more it was as if she were looking down at a huge map of a traffic jam, all the more frenetic for being frozen by the artist. The effect of it was mesmerizing.

She felt herself *slip* sort of sideways, and then she was *in* the painting, amid the frantic rush of the shards of vivid hues. There was brilliant color everywhere and a thing like noise all around her, exciting and scary at the same time. It was a flat, pulsing place, making Geena feel she had been made two-dimensional, the way they did with special effects in movies. Somehow the simplicity of the work made it more intense. The energy of the painting was so great she was starting to have trouble concentrating, and the lack of depth was beginning to make her feel slightly dizzy, like vertigo in reverse. She looked around, hoping to discover a way to leave, retracing her movements back to where she could make out the gallery where the painting hung, where she slipped out the way she had come in—

—and found herself back at the art museum, staring at the Mondrian canvas with more respect than ever before.

It was two weeks later that she tried it again, this time with a lovely, lucid Vermeer of a young woman in an open window reading a letter. Geena let herself in beside the young woman, and stood there, smelling the salt in the cool ocean breeze. The quality of the air itself was glorious. Geena marveled at the preternatural clarity of the light, and the rich, meticulous detail around her, so much sharper than anything recorded by a camera.

The young woman kept on reading her letter, and paid no attention to Geena.

Growing more accustomed to this remarkable place, Geena started down the hallway in the right side of the canvas. She discovered that the rooms beyond kept the same glowing quality of light. The rooms looked narrow and bare to her, and the language—Dutch—sounded like a weird version of German, and she only knew a few words of German, learned from Mister Gronigen at the market. There had to be some way she could make herself understand the words without three years of study. She decided she had to work on it some more, listen more closely.

In the main room of the house, she decided she wanted to leave the painting, but try as she would, she could not make herself slip out of the picture. This was annoying at first, and then frightening. She ended up running through the house, trying to find the place to depart, and hoping she would not be stuck here forever. She didn't want to live in a time with no penicillin, no running water, no television or any kind of electricity, not even batteries for her tape recorder. No travel faster than thirty miles an hour—and only then on fast horses with frequent remounts. Few legal rights for most men and none at all for women. Wars going on all over Europe, at least that's what her history teacher had said. A place with no jeans and no running shoes. No sports programs. No school for girls at all. She wanted to go *home*.

Finally, tears running down her face, and a dread growing within her that she would be stuck in this luminous Dutch world for the rest of her life (however long that might be—What would her parents think? What would the police do? Would she be on *America's Most Wanted*, or one of those shows? Would she end up a mystery?) she stumbled back into the room where the young woman was still reading her letter.

And there Geena slipped out, exactly the way she had come in.

Her whole experience in the painting had taken less than ten minutes but Geena felt she had been gone for the entire afternoon, and it left her shaken, her confidence eroded, and her nerves frayed. She stood in front of the canvas fighting back tears, and vowed that she would never do that again, no matter how exciting she thought the painting might be. It was too risky.

Then came summer vacation.

On rainy summer days Geena Howe liked nothing better than to go to the museum and stare at the huge painting of water lilies. She had done her term report on the Impressionists, and knew a little about Claude Monet, who painted the picture. She liked the way it made her feel, as if the rain was helping to make the painting more real, more alive.

That was very important to Geena, because the fifteen-year-old had begun to realize she had a very special gift. She had never met anyone else who could *think* themselves into paintings. Nothing she had ever read mentioned that ability, either.

It was kind of nice, knowing she was unique. And kind of scary, too. Not just because of what could happen to her in a painting, either, but because if she ever talked about this, who would believe her? She would have to be very convincing for people not to think she was nuts. If she hadn't thought herself into those two paintings, she probably wouldn't think it was possible either.

Now that she had had a couple of months to mull it over, she knew her talent was very special and she would be a fool to waste it. Which meant going into another painting. And another. And another. She would have to do it on her own, telling no one about it until she had enough experience and information that no one could doubt she had done it.

3

It was about one-thirty in the afternoon; rainclouds were gathering over the city, getting ready to release their burdens. It was going to be a dreary day. Geena had finished lunch an hour ago and had decided she would spend the afternoon on a quest.

She would choose a painting she liked, one that looked worth exploring. She had made an agreement with herself: If anything went wrong this time, she would stay out of paintings for the rest of her life. If it went okay, she would make plans for more experiments. This would be her first big adventure, if she didn't lose her nerve. Something as beautiful as this painting of water lilies was a real challenge.

Standing in front of the enormous canvas, she cocked her head to the side and squinted. At this angle, the light reflected off the brushstrokes in a shimmery way, as if the paint itself were moving. And it seemed to her she could see something at the edge of the canvas, just beyond the water lilies. She moved a step nearer the painting. If she looked at the painting *just so* she was certain she could just make out the stones of a castle reflected in the water of the lily pond.

Only it wasn't a pond, now that she inspected it more closely. It was shaped deliberately, curving around the stone flank of a building; the stones were reflected in the water, high walls, massive, with battlements at the top. The water lilies floated on a *moat*, the moat of the castle whose rising bulk she saw just beyond the edge of the canvas. If she were to go into this painting she would need a boat—she certainly wasn't dressed for swimming.

Looking down at the foot of the painting, Geena decided she saw the very end of the prow of a simple, open boat, probably the kind that you poled instead of rowed, because the moat couldn't possibly be that deep. Claude Monet, the artist, must have sat in such a boat, Geena was sure of it. So now it would be her boat. It took a trick of the mind now, a shift in perspective. She would step into the boat, and glide off through the water lilies to the castle with the green-stone walls that stood a little way beyond the painting.

She walked forward, right toward the canvas, and felt the boat tilt under her weight. She reached out for the pole to steady the boat and get her bearings.

Yes. Now that she was in the painting, she saw that the castle was bigger than she had first thought, and probably older too, given the ruined tower that rose on the rear of the castle.

Taking the pole firmly in her hands, she pushed out through the water lilies toward the castle with the ruined tower.

1

As she approached the castle, Geena could see a lady in one of the upper windows. She was dressed in many layers of soft, gauzy fabric cut something like the dresses the medieval virgins wore in her world history book, but far more clinging. The lace insert at her neck was like something Geena's great-grandmother wore instead of the ornaments on the medieval ladies. It made her look odd, a hodgepodge of centuries and fashions. And the hairstyle was all wrong for this kind of castle, consisting of two long, light brown braids hanging down from a frizzy cloud of crimped hair, more like a pre-Raphaelite Madonna of the last century than a true medieval noblewoman.

Now that she was less than twenty feet from the castle, Geena noticed that the lady wore an embroidered garment like a long, heavy-duty apron over her tissue-fine garments. She could not remember seeing anything like it in the museum's collection of altarpieces and other embroidery-work. Finally Geena saw the castle; she noticed that it had towers, three that seemed to have sprung up while she looked away. One was large and round, and the other two a bit smaller. What kind of castle was this? And what kind of lady lived in it?

Taking great care, Geena poled herself over to the edge of the moat where the mossy bank didn't look too steep to climb. Geena was dressed in jeans and a green cotton sweater, and wearing walking shoes—nothing fancy, what she always wore to the museum—but she didn't want to make a mess of herself, either, since she didn't know what she was getting into. Given the way Geena's mother acted when there were guests in the house, it was probably a good idea to try to stay neat. Geena was pretty sure the lady in the castle wouldn't like it if she showed up covered in grass stains and mud, getting the tapestries and the furniture dirty.

She found a length of good rope in the boat, and tied it to the gnarled root of a tree so she could come back to it. That was very important, because Geena had realized in the Vermeer painting that she could only get out of a painting the same way she came in. She knew she had to be very careful to keep her path of departure open and ready, in case she had to leave quickly. She did not know what it would be like to be trapped in a painting, but after what happened in the Dutch house, she was reasonably sure she wouldn't like it, not even in the late nineteenth century, so she took all the precautions she could, going so far as to tie her cardigan around the trunk of the tree to mark the spot for later.

It took a couple of minutes to scramble up the bank to a stand of trees she didn't quite recognize, but had the general shape of weeping willows. The trees had the same blurry look as the water lilies had, and she kept trying to bring them more sharply into focus, but without success. After a little while she gave up and started across the deep green of the lawn to the gate she saw in the castle wall.

As she walked, she whistled her favorite song, and slowly the trees began to sway, as if she had summoned up the wind for them. The air was summer-warm and smelled of developing fruit, as if there were an orchard not far off.

The gate was so weathered that the wood looked as if it would fall apart if Geena hit it too hard. But she knew better than to do this, for there was always the chance that the gate was sturdy. She took hold of the rusty iron latch and tugged on it, hoping it would move without her having to wrestle it open. To her surprise it slid as if it had been oiled that morning.

There was a topiary garden of feathery plants she couldn't identify just inside the gate. Geena closed the gate and stood staring at the garden. Near her, a rooster opened his green, leafy beak to crow. Not far away, a hedge-cat crouched, preparing to jump on a shrubbery rabbit. Geena went a little further into the garden, and stared at the marble fountain that trickled over old marble in the center of the topiary. In the middle of the fountain was a statue of Pan playing his pipes. There were water lilies in the fountain, as there were in the moat. Geena went and sat on the marble rim of the fountain, wanting to take in all the wonders of the garden.

A few minutes later, a servant came out of the castle. He was some sort of page, Geena guessed, probably a couple of years younger than she was, for there was no sign that he had any need to shave yet. He wore livery of a blue-green velvet doublet and long green hose. The velvet was the soft, wrinkly kind that she had often seen in the Victorian ball gowns in the clothing display at the museum. He had a floppy green velvet cap on his shoulder-length, reddish-brown hair. His shoes were something like low jodhpur boots, not like medieval shoes at all. Geena realized he was wearing a costume, as if he were in a play. What sort of place was this, where Victorians dressed up in clothes from the Middle Ages?

"Good gracious!" exclaimed the page as he caught sight of Geena. "What on earth?" He spoke in English but with an attractive French accent.

"Or on canvas," said Geena, and for some reason blushed.

"What?" he demanded, coming toward her with intent curiosity.

"That's what I'm trying to figure out," she said, wishing she didn't feel so clumsy or awkward.

His jaw dropped. "You're a girl."

"Yes," said Geena, puzzled that he should be surprised. "What did you think?"

But he had more questions of his own to ask before he answered hers. "What kind of—why did you—how did you get in here? And who are you? Look at you!" He came up

to her and shook his head in disgust. "Where did you get those terrible clothes? You're not even dressed right for riding. And why in the world is your hair so short?"

"I could ask the same thing of you," said Geena, a little frightened and wanting to hide it, "about having peculiar clothes." She tossed her head and felt her short curls against her face.

"I belong here," he said with the sureness of a cat. "I am Crispin."

"Well, I am Geena," she said, and held out her hand so they could shake, to make the introduction stick.

To her astonishment, Crispin bent and kissed her hand. Now she turned scarlet, and could not think of a thing to say except, "You don't have to do that," even though she decided she kind of liked it.

"Surely you're not expecting me to shake hands as if you were a boy just because you're wearing trousers, do you? What kind of boor do you think I am?" He gave her no time to answer, but went on scolding. "And speaking of your trousers, why are you wearing them? We may be in the country, but that's no excuse. It's hardly proper for a girl to have them on."

"They're not trousers, they're jeans," she said, doing her best to be patient but guessing that Crispin might not accept her answer.

"Whatever you call them, you shouldn't be wearing them. Look at them. They aren't at all suitable. What possessed you to put them on? Why are you wearing them at all?" He had his hands on his hips and he acted as if he was getting angry, the way her young brother did.

"I always wear jeans," said Geena, wondering what strange thing the boy would say next. "Everyone does."

Crispin laughed with disbelief. "I can't imagine what 'everyone' would permit girls to dress so improperly. Whoever they may be, they do not make the rules here. You must get changed at once. It won't do for you to go running around the grounds looking like a gypsy."

"Why? There's nothing wrong with my jeans. I wear them all the time," Geena protested.

"Not here, you don't, or someone would have told us." He shook his head. "You're like something out of a novel about the American West." Suddenly he laughed, throwing his head back the way actors sometimes did in movies.

Now Geena was truly baffled. She could not imagine why this oddly dressed boy would think she was so funny. She turned away from him. "It's not polite to laugh at people."

"It's not polite to go running about the countryside in— what-do-you-call-them?—jeans," he countered; his gaiety fled. "Look, you'd better come inside and put on some proper clothes, or there could be Old Scratch to pay." He glanced around as if he expected this person to appear at once. "Come with me."

"Where are we going?" Geena asked, trying to think what kind of adventure she had got herself into. She knew she was not supposed to go anywhere with strangers, but since she was in a painting, and a beautiful, calm painting at that, what harm could there be? And wouldn't everyone she met be strangers, after all?

"You're going to change into something decent, and then I'll introduce you to my aunt." He had a stubborn set to his chin, and she noticed that he spoke sharply, clipping the ends of his words.

"But . . ." She could think of no objection that would make sense to him. So she tagged along after him, through the garden and into the deep, stony shadow of the castle.

2

They went down a short, narrow hall and into an enormous kitchen, with three open fireplaces set with spits, and two cast-iron ovens flanking them. Light streamed in from a long window high up the wall, making the place glitter and shine. One long, butcher-block table went down the center of the room, and at the far end was a sink with a pump-handle for water. A churn stood beside the table, next to a glass pitcher. A variety of utensils, from cleavers and knives to spatulas and strainers, was hanging from hooks suspended from a long iron bar in the ceiling, where they could be reached easily and quickly.

"Cook's out," said Crispin, with a wave of his hand. "We're having goose tonight, and she's fletching it." He chuckled at the thought. "It's a good, fat goose with plenty of skin to crackle."

But Geena was baffled by one word he had used. "Fletching . . . that has something to do with arrows, doesn't it?" She remembered her brother telling her that he had a badly fletched arrow in his archery class at college. "Why would a cook be making arrows?"

Crispin turned to her, astonished at her question. "It has to do with feathers," he said as if she were five years old and not fifteen. "She's pulling the feathers off the goose. You can't eat it with the feathers still on, can you?"

"I . . . guess not. But wolves do, don't they?" she went on, remembering something she had seen on *Nature*.

"Wolves don't stuff and roast the goose first," said Crispin scornfully. "Who taught you? Your tutors must have been ignorant."

"My teachers," said Geena with heavy emphasis, "are very

good. They just don't waste time on things like . . . like fletching geese."

"Oh?" said Crispin, doubt in every line and inflection. "And what *do* they teach that is so important?"

"Lots of things," she declared. "We have classes in world affairs, and in English composition, and in history, and in algebra, and in biology, and in domestic resources." Geena didn't count gym as a class, though she enjoyed doing a backbend on a narrow board, and playing soccer. She tilted her head up. "Next fall I get to take astronomy."

"Astronomy. Algebra." Crispin laughed, not believing a word of it. "What school do you go to?"

"Washington High." It was her first year there, and she was still a bit overcome with the size and bustle of it, but her grades were good, and she had a few good friends, especially Fiona Daniels (whom everyone called Spike) and Marinelle Hunt (who sat behind her in algebra and domestic resources and lived a block away). They were always hanging out together. She wished they were here right now, to help her deal with this high-handed boy.

"Washington High? That's a silly name for a school, unless it's a church school, of course, or on the high street. Given your clothes, it's probably Washington High Street. I doubt the church schools would let you dress that way, or cut your hair like that, even if you were going into the convent," he said, and abandoned the game he had been playing with her. "Experimental school for females. They encourage every kind of wildness." He shrugged and pointed in the direction of a side room. "That's the laundry. You can find a dress in there, on the rack along the east wall."

"But—" Geena protested.

"Get changed, or I shall have to leave you here. And the next person who discovers you might not be as cordial as I am. What would you do then?" He had one of those smug expressions that boys learn when they are about eleven and never forget. She wanted to yell at him for it, but realized he had made a good deal of sense with his suggestion. Taking a different approach with Crispin, she shrugged as if it meant little to her either way.

"Okay." She saw his lack of understanding in his face and realized he didn't know the word. "Yes. All right."

He was a little surprised at her ready cooperation. "Aren't you going to refuse?"

"Why should I? What you said is reasonable. So I'll do it." She came a step nearer to him. "Tell me, where am I to put my clothes? I don't want anyone taking them."

"I shouldn't worry about that," said Crispin in a superior way that made Geena want to choke him. "Unless one of the servants has a growing son at home, I shouldn't think they'd touch them, let alone take them." He shook his head once. "What sort of girl wears those jeans?"

"All kinds of girls do!" Geena exclaimed hotly. "And I like them. They're comfortable."

"Girls at your Washington High, I suppose? Do your instructors teach you to want to vote, as well?" His smirk was infuriating. "Well, you can at least dress properly while you're here."

"Fine," said Geena, determined to remain on pleasant terms with him until she knew more about what was going on. She had not anticipated dealing with anyone while in the painting. It hadn't happened before.

The laundry turned out to be a large, low-ceilinged room with four big tubs set over a fire-grating in the middle, and another five smaller tubs ranged along the far wall. The air was close and smelled of soap. Geena made her way to the rack, and began to look at the various clothes hung on hooks. All of them had the same slightly blurred appearance of everything else in the painting she had entered. Reluctantly she chose a dress with a high waist, sleeves puffed in three ranks, and a long, full trumpet-cut skirt. The color was a deep, intense green, so dark it was almost black. She got out of her clothes, and hung them on the hook she had taken the dress from, slipped her wallet from her pocket and stuffed it under her bra strap, and then pulled the dress over her head.

There were laces up the back, and no matter how she twisted and turned, she could not find a way to tighten and secure them. Too bad there wasn't a zipper at least, or a loose enough fit that she wouldn't have to bother. She tried bending over forward, and then backward, but neither position made it any easier. After wrestling with the dress and herself for a good five minutes, she gave up and went out of the laundry, calling for Crispin. "I can't get the laces done right," she said.

"Well, of course you can't," said Crispin with heavy sarcasm. "You have a maid for that."

"I do not," said Geena hotly. "It's silly to make dresses you can't get in and out of by yourself."

"If you're a servant, that's probably true," said Crispin grandly. "But if you are a lady, your maid should tend to you." He blushed to the roots of his rust-colored hair. "All right. I'll fasten them for you."

"Thanks." She turned around and felt him struggle with the laces, muttering when the ends of the cord were not even. Finally she heard him give an exasperated sigh. "Is it done?"

"As best I can," he answered, less sure of himself than before. "I didn't tighten it very much."

"Good," said Geena, who thought the bodice was binding her chest worse than her athletic bra. "It's fine, Crispin."

"If you say so," he responded uncertainly. As she turned around, he scrutinized her. "Well, it's an improvement. But your hair . . ."

"What about my hair?" she demanded when he did not go on. She had got it cut not a week ago at Stacy's Clippery, and was proud of the way it looked.

"It's . . . too short," he answered as if he could think of no other way to express his disapproval.

"Too short?" Geena echoed. She had been letting it grow out on top since April and now a wing of it fell across her brow and almost brushed her ear. Lots of her friends had their hair cut short for summer athletics. "Well, yeah, it is shorter than yours. That's what you're saying, isn't it?"

"Never mind, it can't be fixed," he grumbled, and pointed along another one of the stone corridors. "You'll have to come with me. I suppose I'd best introduce you to my aunt."

"Fine," said Geena, squaring her shoulders and standing the way Miz Wilson taught her to do in gymnastics. "Lead the way."

"Well, I have to," said Crispin with a return of his superior manner. "You don't know where anything is."

The castle turned out to be larger than Geena had thought it was at first. She followed along after Crispin, down hallways and through cavernous rooms where the light on the stone constantly changed. At last they went up a broad staircase, and then a narrow one, and Geena found herself in the room where she had seen the lady.

"Crispin," she called out in a sweet, well-modulated voice from her place in the X-shaped chair heaped with pillows. She was fairly slender and rather pale, not quite as old as Geena's mother, by the look at her, though the sense of age might be the lack of make-up and a good bra—she might be as young as thirty, Geena realized. She had a studied indolence about her that made Geena wonder what it was she was trying to prove. "How good of you to come, my dear." Then she noticed Geena. "And who have you there with you?"

"I wish I knew," said Crispin, doing his best to sound ill-used. "I found her a while ago. She was in the back garden."

"Was she?" said his aunt in a very polite but distant way. "How very odd. How did she come there?"

"I don't know," said Crispin, talking as if Geena could neither hear nor speak for herself. "She says her name is Geena."

"I came across the moat, through the water lilies," Geena answered, determined to speak up. "In a boat with a pole."

"Across the moat," said Crispin's aunt. "Why?"

"I was curious about the castle," said Geena.

"Ah," said Crispin's aunt, drawing it out as if it meant more that way. "Not many are. Not many know it's here." She gave a single, slow nod, as if she were bowing.

"I wanted to see it, to find out about it," said Geena, her enthusiasm increasing as she spoke. "I wanted to know *everything*."

"So young, so young," murmured Crispin's aunt with an indulgent smile. Now Geena knew where he got it.

Crispin again expressed his opinion. "She isn't expected so perhaps she shouldn't stay. Aunt Lucrece, what are we going to do about her?"

"I don't know. But you're right—I suppose we will have to do something," she murmured, and stared out the window again. She remained like that a short while, gazing out at a blank place in the air, and then gave her attention to Geena and Crispin once more. This time her question was as crisp as she had been languorous before. "When you say you came across the moat because you were curious, what, exactly, were you curious about?"

"I couldn't see the castle clearly, and I wanted a closer look. It was a reflection in the water lilies. I couldn't see it very well, so I decided to boat over. I didn't think anyone would mind if I did. I didn't want to do anything wrong. Just to be able to find out what it was," said Geena. "I think it's a very interesting place." She hoped that this would put the worst of their suspicions to rest.

"Interesting," repeated Crispin's Aunt Lucrece. "Interesting." She leaned forward and said with great intensity, "Are you sure it wasn't because it is *haunted?*"

3

Geena could hardly believe what she heard. "Haunted? This castle?" She laughed aloud. "Yeah, I bet."

"Don't do that," Crispin urged in an undervoice. "The ghosts will hear you."

"They don't like being made mock of," added Aunt Lucrece. "They can become quite unpleasant if they are not believed."

"How can they?" Geena demanded, looking around in astonishment as if she expected to see a special-effects display. It would be a great place for such a trick. "There's no such things as ghosts."

"Oh, dear," whispered Aunt Lucrece. She patted the largest of the pillows supporting her. "I was afraid you might be one of the doubters."

"If that means I don't believe in ghosts, you're right. I don't." Geena folded her arms and looked directly at Aunt Lucrece. "I'm surprised that you do. Believe in ghosts."

"How can you say that?" demanded Crispin hotly. "You don't know anything about it. You've just got here, and you're talking about things you don't know—"

"I don't have to have been here any time not to believe in ghosts. I don't believe in them at home, so why should I believe in them here?" Geena pointed out reasonably. She was glad that this place wasn't quite real, or all this talk about ghosts might be scary, like something in the movies before the bad guy shows up with a knife or a hatchet and starts chopping.

"So I thought, once," said Aunt Lucrece with a wistful smile. "Before I discovered the ghost."

18

Crispin reached out and laid his hand on his aunt's. "Don't upset yourself. Please, Aunt Lucrece."

"It is all so dreadfully . . . odd," said Aunt Lucrece. "I thought this morning that it would be an eventful day, and here it is barely noon and this young person arrives. What more will happen?" She nodded twice as if to approve her own question. "I dare not speculate."

"I have a name. My name is Geena, Geena Howe," she said, not liking being called "this young person" as if she weren't in the room. "G-e-e-n-a," she added, spelling it.

"Geena is an unusual name," said Aunt Lucrece in an evaluating manner, as if she planned to judge the name in a contest. "I don't know if I have encountered it before, except as a diminutive. And not spelled that way." She looked as if she thought Geena's parents didn't know how to spell.

"It's Japanese for silver-colored," Geena said, lifting her chin. "My parents like Japanese things."

This brought a dawning look of satisfaction to Aunt Lucrece's eyes. "What can have possessed them to give you a Japanese name? Not that it isn't charming, of course, but still . . . Fascinating people, the Japanese. So very cultured, with such fine aesthetic values. I know there are some Japanese prints somewhere in the castle. I've come across them from time to time, though not always in the same place." She made an uncertain gesture indicating most of the building. "My late husband purchased a kimono for me shortly before he died. He came across it in Marseilles, as I recall. It is magnificent." She sighed heavily.

What was it about a kimono that would make this lady so sad? Geena wondered. Was it that her husband had died recently, and so she was still grieving for him? Or was it something else? It would be very rude to ask about these things, so she made herself hold her tongue as much as she wanted to know more. But she had to ask something or she would burst. "How big is this castle? I couldn't see all of it as I came across the moat."

"That's hard to say," Aunt Lucrece answered distantly, a

19

fine frown line between her arched brows. "Some days it is quite large. Others, not so much."

"Oh, sure," said Geena before she could stop herself. "It comes and goes, changing size."

Aunt Lucrece looked directly at her. "Yes. That's it precisely."

It was hard for Geena not to laugh. "And it's haunted."

"Yes," said Aunt Lucrece with a shudder. "Just at present it is fairly large, but by evening, who knows?"

This was more than Crispin could stand. "Look," he interrupted before Geena could speak again, "this is very distressing to my aunt. You are upsetting her. I think you should apologize."

Geena stared at him. "Why?" she asked him. "It isn't as if I want to upset her. I didn't mean to—uh—distress her. She can tell me herself if she doesn't like answering my questions."

"You are a most peculiar girl," said Crispin, making it a condemnation. "No doubt it is the fault of your education. This Washington High where you go to school—though I doubt it actually exists, for even experimental schools are better than what you describe—must be a very strange place, to make you think your behavior is acceptable."

This stung Geena and she glared at him. "Why isn't it acceptable, I'd like to know?"

Now it was Crispin's turn to be flustered. As he spoke, his voice cracked and he sounded very young. "Well, I . . . I don't know what to say to you. You are devoid of proper feeling, and it does not cause you any—"

"Crispin, please, remember," interrupted his aunt, raising an admonishing finger. "This child is a guest in our castle. We are not so lost to propriety that we seek to embarrass her, are we?" She managed a smile so sticky sweet that Geena was reminded of an old-fashioned valentine, with little cherubs holding lace hearts, and pale girls with languishing eyes and elaborate hairdos like pillows. She also did not like being called a child, not at fifteen.

Crispin set his mouth in a firm line. "It's not fitting," he insisted.

"It may not be," said Aunt Lucrece. "But we owe it to Geena to be as cordial as we are able." She looked over her shoulder as she said this, as if she expected to see something unwelcome in the shadows of the tower room.

"What's the matter?" asked Geena, trying to sound polite.

"It's . . . nothing," said Aunt Lucrece faintly, and put her hand to her brow. "Nothing at all."

Crispin made a gesture with his hand which Geena was pretty sure meant "shut up." He reached down and grabbed a silken cushion from a heap of them on the floor. "Here, Aunt Lucrece," he offered, going to her side. "It will make you more comfortable."

Maybe, thought Geena as she watched Crispin tend to his aunt, *maybe Aunt Lucrece has had some kind of breakdown, the way Miz Dunkel had when her family all got killed in a car crash.* That would explain the care Crispin took of her, and his constant concern about upsetting her. It might also explain why she was so languid. Miz Dunkel had been out of school for a whole semester and when she came back to teach again, she seemed worn down and . . . flimsy, sort of the way Aunt Lucrece was, filled with lethargy, and looking dazed. Some of the kids had made fun of Miz Dunkel, but Geena had not thought it was fair to do that. Geena decided to be a little more careful around Aunt Lucrece. "Is there anything I can do to help you?" It was the sort of offer Geena's mother would approve.

"How?" asked Aunt Lucrece in a distant tone. She gazed upward at the patterned-and-beamed ceiling. "What can an upstart girl like you do?"

"I don't know," said Geena, a bit more sharply than she had intended. "That's why I asked you."

Aunt Lucrece regarded Geena with new interest. "Do you mean what you say? That you would be willing to help me? Us?"

"Sure," said Geena, not at all certain it was true as she

21

recalled the panic she had felt in the Vermeer painting when she could not slip out.

Crispin snorted with disbelief as he adjusted the cushion for his aunt. "She doesn't know anything. How can she help?"

"It may be," said Aunt Lucrece, "that because she doesn't know anything she will be able to see our predicament more clearly. Her perspective is not the same as ours, and we should take advantage of it. She may be able to discover some new means of dealing with—"

"The ghost?" suggested Geena, hoping that she had guessed wrong. "I thought we'd covered that."

"Since you don't believe in them," said Crispin sarcastically.

"But don't you see?" said his aunt, looking from Geena to her nephew with a kind of anticipation that made Geena worry. "If she truly does not believe, the hauntings may have no impact upon her. If she is immune, she may be able to keep the castle . . . intact for a change."

"Keep the castle? Intact?" Geena repeated. The words made no sense at all. Why should the castle be in any danger of coming apart? It was made of stone, wasn't it? How could it break up?

"Yes." Aunt Lucrece sighed again. "The haunting comes before a . . . change. If the ghost is seen, it is certain that changes will follow." She put her hand to her bosom. Geena remembered seeing a painting by Sargent of a woman in a white dress who held her hand that way. She had been curious about it, but not curious enough to think herself into it.

"The last time it happened was four weeks ago," said Crispin, sounding very world-weary for such a youngster.

Aunt Lucrece looked toward the window. "You can see out there, in the field. All those wheat stacks. They weren't there before last month. There wasn't even a field, just a vague, shining mist. Like a fuzzy spot in the light. And now it looks as if we are in for a year of harvest." She patted her cloud of frizzy hair in an absent-minded way.

Crispin took up where his aunt left off. "Those wheatstacks are only the latest in a series of developments, and they're mild compared to some of the changes that have taken place here." He made an exasperated sound, and went on as if admitting to a fault of his own. "This morning the castle had five towers. I haven't counted how many it has now, but it's probably six."

Geena was mesmerized. "But . . . how?"

"That is what we hope you can find out, since you have made such a generous offer," said Aunt Lucrece, sounding more business-like than before. Then her languor returned and she added, "Not that any of us expect miracles, of course. Especially from a stranger. Not that I intend any insult. But all of us have tried and failed, so it may be that you are just what we need."

"I see," said Geena, but she was more baffled than ever. She tugged at the enveloping skirt of her dress and wandered over to the window that looked toward the fields. Sure enough, there were rows of wheatstacks in the brilliant sunlight, their color so luminous that the individual stalks glistened. "It's beautiful out there," said Geena, in spite of herself.

Aunt Lucrece began to weep. "Yes, it is. They will change through the afternoon and continue to be beautiful as the day wanes. Yet who knows what will become of them when night has fallen. And what will become of us?" She dabbed at her eyes with a lace handkerchief.

"Aunt Lucrece," exclaimed Crispin, trying to soothe her. He shot a hard look at Geena, saying angrily, "Now look what you've done."

"You were the one who thought I should meet your aunt. You brought me up here," Geena reminded him sharply. "You made me wear this dress."

"And a good thing, too," said Crispin, more sharply than he intended.

Geena's response was silenced by a sound like low thunder. She felt her arms prickle and the hair on her neck rise. She tried not to shiver. She turned slightly and saw a shadow near the opposite window, a shadow that looked like a man in a short jacket with a cravat instead of a tie, wearing a beard and smoking a pipe. There was something in his hand, long and pointed, and for an instant Geena feared the spectre had a gun. It was all she could do to keep from ducking.

"Oh God, preserve us," moaned Aunt Lucrece. "He has returned." She put her slender hand to her face.

Crispin went pale but stood his ground as if determined not to see the figure.

Without doubt, this was the ghost.

"What will happen now?" Aunt Lucrece asked the air, making a point of looking in the opposite direction from the ghost, as if to hide from the shadowy figure. "What will become of us?"

As frightened as she was, Geena was more curious. There was something about seeing a man in the clothes in the style of the late 19th century in this setting of artificial medievalism that intrigued her more than it scared her. Why on earth would he be here? And why were Crispin and his aunt so afraid of him? He didn't seem dangerous. At least, she told herself as she tried to see more than the density of shadow. If she could see him, no matter how awful he looked, it would be better than guessing about a smudge of darkness with vague outlines.

"What terrible thing has he done this time?" asked Aunt Lucrece, taking Crispin's hand for support. "Look around and tell me the worst."

Geena didn't know what she was looking for, but she obediently went to the other window and gazed out. The light was the lovely, luminous light she liked so much in the water lilies painting, like something alive, dazzling. But there was something wrong, she realized, as she surveyed

24

the expanse beyond the window. She blinked and squinted, trying to bring what she saw—or what she did not see—into focus. For a long moment she stared in disbelief, and then a surge of dismay went through her as the enormity of her predicament was born in on her.

The moat with all its water lilies had vanished.

4

Aunt Lucrece glanced out the window and heaved an ill-used sigh. "It's the hour," she said fatalistically. "The angle of the sun has changed."

Doing her best to sound calm, Geena said, "What do you mean? Why would the moat just . . . disappear because of the time of day?"

"It does," said Crispin quietly. "Most of the time the changes occur at about two hour intervals."

"Changes?" Geena repeated, horrified at the possibilities it brought to mind. "You mean the moat might not come back?" She did not want to think what would happen to her if she were stranded here. "What kind of changes are you talking about?"

"There's a cycle," said Crispin with a world-weariness that did not go well with his youth.

"Then it comes back to the same place at least once a day? That's the way it turns out, isn't it?" she asked, feeling the first rush of relief. "The moat isn't gone forever?" She would have to be here through the night, perhaps, but tomorrow there would be a few hours when she could leave.

"Generally the whole pattern is repeated daily, though it's not always the same," was Crispin's vague answer.

"Don't go bothering the girl with all these calculations," his aunt expostulated. "It's too provoking to have to realign one's life every two hours or so, day in and day out."

"I should think so," Geena said with feeling. She began to wonder what time it was in the museum. How long had she been gone? Had anyone noticed yet that she was missing? And what would they do about it? How would they go about finding her? Or could they find her at all? Her mom expected her home at four-thirty, and she had soccer at seven in the evening, when it was cooler, if it was dry enough after the rain. Was she going to end up here for the rest of her life? With no soccer, no comic books, no TV, no computer, no microwave, no movies, no friends, no school, no parents, no brother, no *anything*? Just this stupid castle that changed every two hours? She made herself take a long, slow breath, count to ten and let it out for a count of five.

"You're looking a bit pale, Geena," said Aunt Lucrece. "Shall I send Crispin for my smelling salts?"

"What for?" Geena asked.

Aunt Lucrece gave her an indulgent smile. "Why, to restore you, of course. If you are about to swoon, it would be—"

"I *never* swoon," said Geena with disgust. That wasn't entirely true, she thought at once. There was that cute new guy in Miz Hamilton's world affairs class. She could almost swoon for him. She felt herself blush.

"You're better," Aunt Lucrece announced. "The color is returning to your cheeks. Thank goodness. I would hate to have you endure any misfortune on our account greater than what you have already." She reached out a languid hand and plucked at the folds of Geena's skirt. "And how I wish I could explain this place to you, so it would not be so bothersome."

"I wish you could, too," said Geena sincerely. She would have to understand it a great deal better than she did if she were going to find her way out of here.

Crispin looked out the window and shook his head. "It's probably moved around to the south side of the castle."

"What do you mean, moved around?" Geena demanded, not liking anything she was hearing.

"From time to time the moat . . . shifts. In the late afternoon it often goes to the south side of the castle." He made a gesture of helplessness. "Other times it just . . . vanishes."

The cold that struck at Geena then was deep in her bones. "But it comes back, doesn't it?" She could hear her

27

voice rise as she asked the question and hated herself for indulging her fear so much.

"Usually," said Crispin, his attitude so fatalistic that Geena wanted to kick him. "At least it has so far."

"Hardly a morning dawns," said Aunt Lucrece in her best die-away delivery, "that the moat is not once again on the north-east side of the castle. It disappears into the west and moves to the south, as Crispin says, in the afternoon."

"Moats don't do that," Geena insisted. She would have to be more careful about watching for her chance than she had first supposed. The moat would have to be in the same place as it was when she arrived. And what about the water lilies? Would they still be in the moat? She thought it likely that the water lilies would have to be in place for her to be able to get out—after all, the painting she was in was called *Water Lilies.*

"This one does," said Aunt Lucrece with a mixture of resignation and pride.

"During the winter," Crispin volunteered, "the moat keeps to the south most of the time. The ice on it shines like metal in the winter."

It was tempting to call them both crazy, but Geena was afraid that she would offend these two, and she would need their help before her adventure here was done. She kicked at the long hem of her skirt—how binding this mass of cloth could be!—and longed for her jeans so she could go exploring on her own. But that might get her into worse trouble than she was in already. She decided she would have to go along with Crispin and his aunt for the time being, so she said, "What kind of help do you need, that I could do for you?"

Crispin chuckled. "You wouldn't want to try it."

"Why not?" Geena demanded hotly. "And don't tell me it's because I'm a girl."

"But you are a girl," said Crispin at his most infuriating. "And you are not ready to explore the strange parts of the castle, are you? Not knowing so little about this place." He started to pace the room, and then stopped. "I wouldn't venture into certain wings of this castle at any time, not if the rest of the place were on fire."

"Isn't that a little extreme?" Geena asked, thinking that he was being very foolish.

"It may seem that way to you," he responded stiffly. "But there are wings of this castle that vanish regularly and when they reappear they are never quite the same. Would you take a chance of being changed along with the stones?"

"The ghost does all that?" said Geena in polite disbelief.

"Yes, he does," Aunt Lucrece said in a rush of emotion. "And you should not underestimate what it could do to you."

"I'll try not to," Geena said, hoping she could keep from laughing. "Is there a dormouse around here who'll sing 'Twinkle, twinkle, little bat'? And when do they serve the tea, the Mad Hatter, and the March Hare?" This was feeling more and more like something out of *Alice in Wonderland*, and she wondered idly if she, too, like Alice had fallen asleep and this was a dream as fantastical as anything thought up by Lewis Carroll.

"Oh, dear," murmured Aunt Lucrece. "You're not going to succumb to hysteria are you, Geena? For I can't endure dealing with hysterics."

"I am not having hysterics," said Geena making herself speak calmly and quietly. "I am just getting tired of being thought a wimp because Crispin here will not let me help him explore the castle."

"Wait a minute," said Crispin nervously. "I don't want to explore the castle any more than you do."

"But I want to," said Geena. "I want to very much."

"How can you?" Aunt Lucrece demanded of the air, and turned her head away.

"I want to because I'm fascinated by this place. I've read a little about it, and this is my chance to explore. I've never been anywhere like it before," she said enthusiastically. Then, in a softer voice, she admitted, "And I'm afraid I'll be stuck here forever if I don't."

For once Crispin's expression was sympathetic and serious. He came and faced her. "I know how you feel. That's why I think you ought to be careful exploring this place. If anything more happens to you . . ." He smacked his palms together. "We may not have invited you here but we know what our obligations as hosts are."

"Then come with me," Geena pleaded, trying to make the best of an awkward situation. "If you think I can't handle it alone, stay with me."

Crispin looked over at his aunt as if seeking her advice. She pointedly ignored him. He stared up at the ceiling as if he expected to find an answer written there. Then he rubbed his hand across his brow as if he had a headache, and he said, "I'll probably regret this, but all right, I'll go exploring with you. I am curious about this place, I admit it. But—" he held up an admonishing finger— "don't blame me if we get into trouble."

"I won't," said Geena, too elated to quibble about such things. She glanced at the door. "When do we start?"

He frowned with concentration. "We'd better get bread and cheese from the kitchen. We might not find any food in the rest of the castle. And we'll need wraps in case we're stranded for the night."

"Do you think we might?" Geena asked, trying not to feel upset at the prospect. What would happen at the museum if she was gone so long? Or did time happen the same way here? Her science teacher last year, Mr. Rose, had said that in space time slows down. You could be in space for a year, but on earth fifty years had gone by. Maybe the same thing happened in paintings, only in reverse. Maybe a day in a painting was only a couple of minutes in the museum. She sure hoped so.

"What are you thinking about?" Crispin demanded.

"Nothing," she said, knowing it was useless to try to explain it to him. People a hundred years ago didn't think about going into space, or if they did, they got it wrong.

"It doesn't look like nothing," said Crispin, his expression set.

Geena tossed her head. "Let's get the food. And some water. We're going to need that no matter what." Her gym teacher was always telling them not to get thirsty.

"All right," said Crispin, his expression suspicious.

This wasn't getting them anywhere, Geena decided. So she changed the subject as she fell in beside Crispin. "What part of the castle changes the most?"

"Do be careful, you two," Aunt Lucrece called after them as they left her room. "Come back safely."

"The south wing," said Crispin at once, ignoring his aunt's farewell. "More things happen there than any other part of the castle."

"Do you know why that is?" Geena asked. They had reached the staircase and Geena noticed there was a huge tapestry hanging from a balcony above it. It depicted a group of medieval ladies in a gigantic maze that was tipped at an impossible angle. Had that been there before, or was it something new since her arrival?

"The ghost has something to do with it, that's all I know," said Crispin, his chin up to show her he was insulted by her question.

"Tell me more about this ghost," Geena encouraged him. "I've never seen a ghost, except in movies and TV. I don't know what they're like." Too late, she realized she should not have mentioned electronic things.

"So you *do* know about ghosts," Crispin exclaimed, rounding on her. "Though those inventions are new to me. Something American, I should think."

"I don't really know about ghosts. Only as special effects," said Geena, determined not to be side-tracked with explanations that would lead nowhere.

"That means you have to believe in them," Crispin insisted. "You said you didn't, but you do."

"Not the way you mean," Geena said, adding, "Look, this isn't getting us anywhere. We're going to need to make some plans if the south wing is as dangerous as you say it is." She wanted to sound unafraid, but she became a little breathless as she talked, and she knew it was from fear.

"Plans won't do you a lot of good, not if the south wing changes while we're there." He sounded discouraged now, as if he were losing heart before they had begun. "I guess you know what you want, though."

"I want to find out what's happening," she said, not adding that until the moat and water lilies returned, she could not get out of the painting and back to her own time and place. "Does the kitchen change very often, or is it still down that hall?" she asked, pointing in the direction they had come.

"It should be there." He shrugged. "If you're so determined to do this, let's get it over with." With that he led the way into the kitchen, pointing to the pantry. "I'll get the basket. You get the food." He pointed to an array of wicker baskets on a shelf near the door. "Which size do you want?"

Right now, Geena missed her backpack more than she could say. She studied them. "Better make it two. One will be too hard to carry if we fill it. We can spread the load better with two."

"All right," he said, willing to agree with her to that point.

Geena went into the pantry. There were half a dozen loaves of bread that smelled wonderfully fresh. She took two of these and set them on the chopping block table in the middle of the room, then resumed her exploring. She had to keep in mind they might need something more than lunch. If they were caught in the south wing when it changed, they would need something for dinner, and breakfast as well, she supposed.

There were a number of cheeses of different colors and odors set out along two shelves, and a tub of something that smelled like sour cream; Geena took three of the cheeses, and decided that they would need butter as well. They would not have margarine here. People a hundred years ago— now—didn't worry about fat grams or cholesterol or any of

32

that stuff. They ate because they were hungry and their food tasted good. There were pots of fruit preserves on the shelves. Hoping she had translated the labels correctly, Geena took the ones marked *pêche, abricot,* and *framboise.* She was pretty sure these were peach, apricot, and strawberry, but she wasn't completely certain. Her mother once warned her that English and French look enough alike to be misleading.

She found some small, hard sausages in a string draped over a hook, and after a brief hesitation, she took them. Sausages were supposed to store well, though she knew they had a lot of salt and fat. Still, she liked all those Italian picnic sausages that some places put on pizzas.

At the thought of a pizza, her mouth watered and she realized she was getting very hungry. What she wouldn't give right now for a pizza and a big glass of orange juice! She saw a bowl of small, pear-shaped tomatoes, and decided she ought to take a couple of them, too.

The pile on the butcher-block table was growing. She would have to be careful, or the baskets would weigh too much to be carried. Making up her mind, she took a crock of pickles from one of the lower shelves, and decided that would be the last. Looking around, she realized they would need forks and knives, plates and cups and napkins. They would have to be real plates and napkins. There were no paper or plastic plates being used in this time.

"Hey, Crispin," she called out. "Bring those baskets in here and we'll load up."

Crispin appeared in the doorway, a green bottle clutched by its narrow neck in one hand, the baskets in the other. He held up the bottle. "I've got this and another of water. Don't forget." He held them out.

"What is that?" Geena inquired as she sorted out plates and utensils for them.

"Wine, of course," said Crispin. "It's local, not too bad. Better for you than the well-water hereabout."

Geena nodded once. "Right," she said. "Wine." After

everything they were taught about not drinking, here was a kid about her own age telling her that the wine was safer than the water.

"The water's bottled. It's from a safe spring. You can trust it," Crispin told her, as if her hesitation was due to the water and not the wine.

She remembered something her American history teacher, Miss Gunn, had told the class last year—that safe drinking water was fairly new, and one of the reasons people in the past had drunk wine and beer so much was because it was safer than water. Maybe that was true here, too. "Okay," said Geena.

5

Both baskets were full, and, Geena realized as they made their way along the main gallery toward the south wing, uncomfortably heavy and awkward. It would have been a lot easier with a backpack. She felt the strain in her shoulders as she lugged the loop-handled basket, leaning away from the weight to try to improve her balance. Only the realization that it was no easier for Crispin made the effort seem worthwhile.

"How much farther?" asked Geena, thinking they must have covered half a mile worth of stairs and corridors.

"Not much farther, I don't think," said Crispin vaguely. "It should be around here." He waved with his free hand, indicating the cavernous, long room they were traversing on the second floor, going along the long balcony toward the massive wooden door at the end.

"This place doesn't look much like the rest of the castle," said Geena. "It seems, I don't know, older maybe."

"It changes," said Crispin, hitching a shrug. "Sometimes it looks very Italian, sometimes it looks the way it does now, early medieval." He stared at the ceiling. "The fan-vaulting doesn't fit with the rest; it's more English in style than French, and out of period as well." He indicated the beautiful carving in the ceiling. "That's sixteenth century. This stonework is twelfth century. The ghost—"

"What about the ghost?" Geena inquired a bit too sweetly.

"Sometimes when the ghost changes things, he mixes them up. I don't know why." They had reached the huge door. "Look at this," he went on by way of example. "The carving style is German, but the iron-work is Spanish."

"How do you know?" Geena demanded. It all looked

about the same to her. "Never mind that now," she added, seeing he was about to give her a lecture on hinges and wood-carving. "Tell me later. When we're having lunch."

"All right," he said huffily.

Geena saw she had hurt his feelings. "I didn't mean to offend you, Crispin. You can explain it all when we're in the south wing. Okay?"

"All right," he said, his back very stiff. He shoved back the iron bolt holding the door closed, then pulled on it to get it to open.

To Geena's surprise there was no creaking and groaning of the hinges, just the soft shriek of metal on metal, as if the hinges needed oil. The door was ponderous enough, moving slowly because of its weight. The mass of it was impressive. Not even the art museum had such doors. Beyond was another extensive gallery, similar to the one they had just crossed, but different as well. This one had spiral-shaped pillars and a section of the roof was open to the sky.

Crispin sighed. "It's the ambulatory."

"The what?" she asked. She had a vague recollection of hearing the word before, but could not place it.

"It means that the south wing is a monastery right now, the way it is sometimes. For a while last week it was an oast house, and a month ago it was a barn," said Crispin as if Geena were a little kid. "I like the ambulatory best. This is the place where the monks are supposed to walk and meditate. It comes from the Latin word for walking."

"You mean there are *monks* here, too?" Geena demanded. Who else were they apt to encounter on their explorations?

"Probably not," said Crispin, looking around before he closed the big door behind them. "I haven't seen them very often. There aren't very many . . . presences here; I don't think the ghost likes them. There's just the ambulatory, with all the shadows, and the shine off the twists in the pillars. Once in a while I hear the chanting." He led the way along the long balcony. "We'd better get through here quickly. The light is already leaving the courtyard, and that means it

36

could change at any second." He was doing his best not to look scared, and Geena decided for the first time that he was pretty brave to bring her here.

"Where are we going now?" Geena asked as Crispin hurried her along the gallery.

"To the end of this, I hope," he answered. "There should be stairs leading into a round tower. At least there have been before." He lowered his voice. "The ghost sometimes stays around the tower, when it's here."

Geena listened and hoped she could make sense of what he was saying a little while later. She shifted her basket from the right to left hand and lengthened her stride. She was sorry now she had given up her jeans, no matter how scandalous they seemed to Crispin. Her skirts were slowing her down, getting in her way.

"That's the passageway, up ahead," said Crispin. He, too, was a little short of breath. "When we get into it, go up the stairs when you come to them."

"Okay," she answered.

"What is that word, anyway?" he asked her. "That *okay* you say?"

Geena was taken aback. She thought everyone in the whole world understood what *okay* meant.

Sure, she reminded herself. Everyone in the world she came from did, but back here, a century ago, very few people outside of America had heard it. "It means fine, and correct, and everything is normal, and things are going well—like that."

"Is it Chinese?" he asked.

"Actually," said Geena, as she strove to recall what her English teacher Miz Benson had said, "I think it's supposed to be Cherokee Indian. My teacher said it means something like *we agree*. I don't know if that's all true or not."

"Ah," said Crispin with a knowing nod, as if having the word identified with Indians was enough to explain it. "Cherokee. I have heard of these people. They are the ones who write, aren't they?"

Geena looked shocked. "All Indians write," she said with heat. "Even the ones on reservations have schools."

"Yes, yes, they must do," said Crispin, so soothingly that Geena longed to scratch him for being such a stuck-up, old-fashioned, racist, chauvinistic prig. She remembered hearing her mother use that word for the librarian who was fired last year, a prig. She thought it sounded right for Crispin. "You better get ready for the stairs. It's a very long way up."

"I'm ready," said Geena.

"I mean," said Crispin with so much patience that he might as well have been baby-sitting, "that you had best get a hold of your skirts so you can climb without tripping."

"I could do that better if you'd let me keep my jeans on," said Geena sharply, even as she got a handful of her skirt and tugged at it, trying to find a way to hold it so she could move more easily. It was trickier than it looked.

"Possibly," he allowed. "But they are not appropriate."

"As if that matters," said Geena, her temper nearly getting the better of her. Between her clothes, the basket, and Crispin, this adventure was becoming more of an effort than she thought it would be. If she had not been so anxious about getting home, she might have refused to cooperate with Crispin any more.

"Once we're in the tower, we'll have to go quickly. It wouldn't do to be trapped on the stairs during the change, you know." He glanced at her.

"This gallery is longer than it looks," said Geena, not willing to let him scare her.

"Many things in this castle are," Crispin responded, and added in encouraging tones, "Once we're at the top of the tower where can have lunch. The view is very good—when there is a view."

This last cryptic observation caught her attention. "It could be foggy? Is that what you mean?"

"No. I mean everything around the castle could be gone." He said nothing more as he blushed. Apparently he was ashamed to have said so much. "It's still early enough that I don't think we have anything to worry about."

"Good." With satisfaction Geena saw they had at least reached the entrance to the tower. Mindful of what Crispin had told her, she took a good grip on the basket and her skirt and readied herself for the ascent.

The staircase proved daunting: made of rough stone, many of them worn or deliberately uneven, the stairs were steep and narrow, and there was no banister, not even a railing to protect a climber. The wind moved through it constantly, moaning softly to itself. The staircase corkscrewed upward, giving the impression of vanishing into nothingness in perfect three-point perspective. What occasional splashes of light there were came from narrow slits of unglazed windows set at about twelve-foot intervals along the walls, making the gloom seem darker in contrast to the luminous light. All that was missing, Geena decided, was the howl of wolves, or a sudden rush of bats. Which probably happened once the sun went down, when you could no longer see where you were going. *That*, thought Geena unhappily to herself as she made her way precariously toward the top, *was probably what Crispin meant when he said this wasn't a good place to be during one of the changes*, for she supposed she might have had to climb forever if that happened. She didn't like that idea at all.

But finally there was an irregular slice of light overhead, and the dimness brightened into the soft, beigy glow of afternoon. The tower no longer appeared to be an endless stone tunnel, and now gave promise of something quite remarkable.

Like most girls her age, Geena had been at the top of several skyscrapers, but she had never gone to the top of a castle tower. This would be unlike anything she had seen before, she was sure of it.

Now they had nearly reached the upper platform that led out onto the wide towertop. Geena had stopped talking twenty steps earlier, saving her air for the climb. She had to concentrate on everything she did, making sure she did not miss her footing, for a fall from this height in a stone building would surely be fatal, and there was nothing to hang onto if she should happen to fall. She took a little satisfaction in realizing that even Crispin was panting as they made their way up the last few steps.

"It's taller . . . than usual," he told her as they reached the arch opening. "Go . . . right through . . . there."

"Thanks," said Geena, her arms aching from carrying so much up the long flight of stairs. Her calves were as shaky as if she had just played a hour of fast soccer, and when she took a deep breath her chest was tight from the long climb. Relieved that the climb was behind them, Geena stepped through the arch and onto the towertop.

Overhead were smudges of clouds, and spread out around her for as far as she could see were the lush rolling hills adorned with fields and villas that she had seen in so many paintings. No wonder Monet had loved this countryside so much. It was spectacular. The whole scene was imbued with a gauzy lume that reminded her of the way romantic movies used to be shot. The colors were as fascinating and complex as anything she had seen before. Staring, she put her basket down and did a full circle, looking at the scene around her.

"What do you think?" said Crispin, his pride flavored by a little uncertainty. He set his basket down beside hers and was content to watch her admire the place.

"I think it's *beautiful*," Geena answered, her eyes sparkling more than the glints from the water on the river below. She went over by one of the high parts of the battlements. She leaned against the stone and looked down toward the base of the tower that seemed to be very far away. She pulled herself tight against the stones, as if afraid of falling. "At least there's some protection up here, too. Better than coming up the stairs."

"Those are crenelations," said Crispin, showing off his knowledge. "That's what you call them."

"Whatever they are, they're great," said Geena, patting the stonework with affection. They made her feel safe up here at the top of the castle.

"They're to keep the sentries and soldiers hidden from an enemy besieging the castle," said Crispin. "And it gives something to shoot from behind. Arrows, not guns or canon. Sometimes they poured boiling oil on the enemy," he added with ghoulish delight, as if this was his favorite defense.

"I know that," said Geena, unimpressed with his attempt to gross her out, and went back to staring out at the magnificent countryside. "It's alive with light," she said after a long silence.

"Yes, it is, when it's like this." There was a guarded note in his voice, and although he, too, admired the scenery, he did it more cautiously than Geena did. "You wouldn't like it at other times."

"You mean when the ghost is here?" She made a wave of her hand to show the prospect of hauntings did not frighten her. "This is a great place for a picnic, ghost or no ghost," Geena approved, and came back to the basket. "It's the best place for a picnic I've ever seen." Now that she had mentioned food, she was amazed how hungry she was, considering she'd had lunch less than three hours ago. *Three hours and a hundred years ago,* she reminded herself.

Crispin looked about uneasily. "All right," he said after checking the view thoroughly. "I think we have time for it."

"You like being mysterious, don't you?" Geena challenged as she sat down and opened her basket.

"I'm not mysterious. You are," he said with a renewal of that unctuous confidence she had already learned to dislike. "You arrive here completely unannounced, dressed like someone from a pantomime. You behave as if you learned your manners on the moon. You talk about things that don't make any sense, and then you chide me because parts of this castle change from time to time."

"It's not fair," Geena agreed as she sat down and opened the nearer basket.

41

She had been wrong about the *framboise:* it was raspberry, not strawberry, but she didn't mind. It was not as sweet as the jams and jellies she was used to, but this did not trouble her. Spread on bread with butter and cheese, it made a great sandwich, with a taste so rich it seemed to rush out to you before you got it into your mouth.

Crispin had cut slices of pickles and put them with sausages, cheese and butter, and was drinking some of the wine to wash it down. He held a piece of his sandwich to her. "Try this. I think you'll like it. The pickles have mustard seeds and coriander in the brine."

Geena was not sure what that meant, but she good-naturedly took what he offered. The sausages were not as fatty as she had expected—dense with meat and spices she could not identify, and a smoky flavor that reminded her of her mother's New Year's ham. The pickles did have a mustardy taste that was pleasantly tangy and the cheese was darker, more like cheddar than the one she had chosen for herself. She would have to find out what it was called. She chewed with gusto. "That's good," she said when she had finished. "But it's a little dry."

They were seated together on the wide expanse of the tower top, about half-way between the guard station near the center and the crenelations at the edge.

He held out a cup to her and offered her wine. "It aids the digestion," he pointed out. "And a sip or two won't make you lose your head, not so long as you're eating. Food absorbs a lot of the fumes."

"I don't think so, thanks anyway," she said. "Not with those stairs to have to go down. I want to keep my wits about me." If ever she had seen a place that needed a designated driver—or walker—it was that staircase. She was also beginning to wonder if she would have to find an outhouse soon. It was probably useless to hope there was indoor plumbing in a castle.

He held out the water bottle to her. "Then this."

"I don't think so," she said, feeling uncomfortable. If she had to, she thought she could hold it for another hour or so.

He laughed, understanding her predicament. "There's a privy just inside the arch. You can still use it."

She stared at him in surprise. "All the way up here?"

"Why not? What do you think the moat was for? They didn't use it just to stop the enemy, you know. There's a stone seat with a hole in it over the moat. Soldiers and sentries used to use it all the time. They couldn't very well go running down those stairs to the necessary house in the middle of the watch or a battle, could they?" He met her stare with one of his own.

"I guess not," she said after a brief moment of embarrassment. "Thanks."

"Don't mention it," he said, and began to make himself a second sandwich. He had finished smearing butter on a section of bread when he stopped and lifted his head, his eyes narrowing with worry. "Listen," he whispered.

Geena glanced around, aware that a few thin clouds, like fragile veils, had altered the clarity of the light, making it less intense. She didn't hear anything. "What is it?" she asked softly.

"It's changing," said Crispin, only slightly louder than before. "Be careful."

"Of what? What kind of change?" asked Geena, no longer willing to lower her voice. "What's the matter?"

"It's going to . . ." He made a gesture with his hand, and pointed away toward the distant fields.

The wheatstacks were gone, and a whole section of hills had vanished as if into a mist.

Geena stared, hardly daring to breathe. Her eyes were

bright with interest that verged on dread. "Where did they go?"

"I don't know," Crispin admitted, and continued to butter his sandwich bread. "They'll probably be back when the weather is clearer. Those wheatstacks are here only when it is completely sunny. With those high clouds coming, who knows what will happen to the castle." He selected another sausage and split it, laying it on the bread with care, doing his studious best to appear unconcerned, though Geena noticed his hands shook. "Most of the hills go away in the rain."

"And the castle?" Geena asked, worried in spite of her curiosity.

"It gets much smaller." He indicated the tower where they sat. "This usually remains, but not always."

"Oh," said Geena, and felt her appetite desert her. "How much smaller?"

He shrugged in an attempt to show how little the prospect bothered him. "It varies."

She decided he was completely serious, which dismayed her. "Isn't there anything we can do?" Her food no longer interested her. Suddenly her very existence seemed questionable, and that ruined her appetite. She remembered there were two smaller towers at this end of the castle when she first saw it—what had become of them?

"If we could change the sky, it might make a difference," he said distantly. "The light is what makes the difference for the castle."

"How do we change the sky?" she demanded in a burst of impatience that was intended to conceal her own sudden fright.

"I don't know." He took a bite of his new sandwich and chewed with determination, drinking a little of the wine before he swallowed and said, "I don't think the ghost knows how to change the sky, either."

"Oh," said Geena, trying to sound as if she believed him. "Then the ghost can't really do everything."

Crispin didn't give her a direct answer. Instead, he pointed out to where many of the features of the countryside around them were fading, becoming insubstantial as fog, and then fading away altogether to a kind of grey blankness. "That's what the ghost does."

For the last hour and more, Geena had been able to banish her fear from her mind—the fear that she might be trapped forever in this strange place beyond the water lilies. Now the fear rushed in on her with renewed force and she had to make herself take deep, steady breaths, the way the coach told her to do when she had been playing too hard at soccer. She reached for the water bottle and took a long swig of it. She fought the impulse to pant.

"Here," said Crispin, holding out the wine bottle. "This is better."

All the warnings she had been given over the years were now a chorus in Geena's mind. She shook her head and held up her hand to show her refusal.

"Don't be silly," said Crispin primly. "Americans might not drink much wine, but this is France. A sip will not kill you and it will help you to remain calm. Right now that's the most important thing." He put the neck of the bottle into her hand. "Just the one sip. And then have more water, if you must." From the mulish set of his jaw it was apparent he would not permit her to refuse. "Go ahead," he urged.

Feeling brave and guilty at once, Geena obeyed. The lack of sweetness in the taste of the wine was not pleasant, but it did go well with all the flavors of the food she had eaten, more than even a Coke would. At the thought of Coke, she very nearly burst into tears, for if she could not leave this place, she would never taste it again. She swallowed the wine and felt it warm her against the chill that had nothing to do with the warmth of the day. As she prepared to have a little more to eat, Geena made herself ask a calm question. "You said the castle gets smaller. I guess it's something like—out there." She pointed to the grey smudge where the fields had been.

"That's what it looks like," said Crispin. "I don't know what is or isn't there." He coughed once. "And I don't want to find out."

"Is that where the ghost is?" Geena pursued. She was becoming more curious now that she had stopped herself from losing it over missing a soft drink. It was time for her to *do* something, to get off her rear end and find out what was going on in the painting, so she could find her way out once again.

"Probably," said Crispin at his haughtiest best. "I haven't investigated."

"Why not?" Geena demanded. "Don't you want all this to stop?"

"Not if I have to vanish with the building, I don't," said Crispin emphatically.

Geena shook her head in disapproval. "No wonder you get trapped like this—you haven't learned anything about it."

"Oh, and I suppose you expect to go into the . . . whatever that is, and tell the ghost to put it back the way it was?" he retorted, stung. "What a foolhardy, insolent thing to do."

She tossed her head and got to her feet. "Why not? It could work."

"And it could be the end of you forever," said Crispin, sounding worried now instead of miffed.

"Maybe," she admitted quietly. "But if I'm stranded here, it's the end of me, anyway, so I might as well take a chance and try to—"

"There!" Crispin cried out, and pointed to the part of the castle they had come through to reach the tower. Now the gallery and ambulatory were little more than hazy outlines, as if they were lost in a fogbank. "I told you it gets smaller." There was a kind of grim triumph in his pleasant face. "The distance between the tower and the keep changes, too, sometimes."

"What on earth causes that?" asked Geena, too astonished to be frightened.

"The ghost." He crossed his arms as if to protect himself from sudden cold.

"And the tower?" She did not attempt to conceal her nervousness.

"That stays here, like the part in the front. They've never vanished, though they do change a little." He wanted to sound confident and experienced, and managed only to convince Geena that he was more frightened than she was—which was saying a lot.

"Why does it stay here? Why doesn't the tower vanish?" She was asking herself more than him.

"I don't know!" he shouted at her, and then looked away, flushing at his outburst. "I . . . didn't mean . . ."

Much as she wanted to show him up for letting his nerves get the better of him, she stopped herself in time. "I know you didn't," she said in a tone that was almost an apology. "And I didn't mean anything mean by asking about . . . the ghost." Now that she had said it as if she believed it she felt much stranger than she had before.

"Okay," said Crispin, pronouncing the two syllables with great care.

"Okay," Geena seconded. Then she turned abruptly and ran for the guard station, hoping she would find the privy in time.

7

Descending the staircase took almost as long as going up it. Though the baskets were lighter than before, Geena found keeping her balance trickier as she made her way down the uneven steps to the archway through which they had come.

"Well? What do you think?" asked Crispin as they stared out into the filmy nothingness beyond.

"I think we need to get on solid ground," said Geena seriously. "I don't know what will happen if we try to walk through that. And I don't want to fall."

"Certainly not," said Crispin. "It's another two stories down to the ground, though, and it gets a lot darker."

Geena looked down and wished she had thought to get some candles while they were in the kitchen. *Too late now,* she reminded herself. She took a firmer hold on the basket handle and nodded toward the continuing spiral of stairs. "I suppose we'd better get going, before my muscles get stiff." The climb down had put more strain on her than she had expected. She felt the kind of ache in her legs she usually got after her first ballet class at the end of summer vacation, when she would get to the bottom of a *grand plié* and feel as if she would never again stand upright—she would have to hop through life like a frog. Come morning she was sure her muscles would complain every time she moved. But right now she had to keep going, or spend the night here, on the edge of a stone doorway to *The Twilight Zone*. She lowered her head and ordered her eyes to focus on the steps.

Crispin followed after her in silence, his basket held in a white-knuckled fist.

The tower was wider near the base than it had been at

the top, but that offered little relief to Geena, for the light was soon so low that they had to feel their way down the last twenty-six steps, coming to a halt by a stout wooden door held closed by a massive bolt fixed through iron staples into a opening in the stones. It was a door designed to resist catapulted stones and battering rams.

"Can you get it open?" asked Geena as she peered through the gloom at the formidable door.

"I don't know," said Crispin. "If the iron isn't too rusty and the wood of the bolt isn't swollen, perhaps I can." He did his best to convince her as well as himself as he felt the wooden door. "There's a ring at the far end."

"Is that good or bad?" Geena was suspicious of the place, and did her best not to let it show too much.

"It could be either," said Crispin. "If they used the ring to hitch the bolt to a winch, then it's bad. If they used a lever through it, then it's good."

"Let's hope it uses a lever then, or that we can make a lever work," said Geena, determined not to let this place get the better of her now. Judging from the few spills of light from the slit windows, it was pretty late in the afternoon. She wondered fleetingly if the museum were still open, and if so, if she had been missed by anyone. What would her mother do when she didn't show up on time?

"Well, see if you can find something to use for a lever," said Crispin impatiently, as if he had already said something else to her.

"Sorry," she answered, and began to look about the floor for anything they could use as a lever. At last she came upon a kind of closet with rusted weapons inside it, one of which was a lance on a long wooden pole, the kind her history teacher had said was used more than three hundred years ago in the Thirty Years' War. She hefted the shaft and thought the wood felt flimsy. But the lance part, about eighteen narrow inches of steel, seemed strong enough to work like a crowbar. She held her find out to Crispin. "How's this?"

He seemed skeptical as he took it into his hands, but then he grinned. "I think it'll do," he said, and putting the lance's point through the ring, pressing hard at the far end of the metal to try to budge the bolt.

"I can help you," said Geena, and got on the other side of the lancepoint, and tugged as Crispin pushed.

The wood groaned like something out of a Lovecraft story, and the lancepoint began to bend under the pressure.

"Should we stop?" asked Geena, her breathing hurried.

"Not yet." Crispin was panting with effort, but continued his dogged efforts.

The wooden bolt shuddered, howled, and then slid back, making the whole door vibrate. The release came so quickly that both Geena and Crispin nearly fell over.

"Great going," said Geena as she struggled to stay upright. She touched the door, noticing that it opened outward. She leaned on it, and was startled when, with a screech from the unoiled hinges, the door swung open into the place the ambulatory had been.

There were small stone mounds and bits of ruined walls stretching back toward the main part of the castle. In the failing light, the whole place looked insubstantial.

"Most of the place used to be a ruin, except for the part where Aunt Lucrece lives, and the tower. Since the ghost came, the ruin is . . . different," Crispin said as if telling her a dire family secret.

"No kidding," said Geena. She looked into the haze and tried to make out the walls of Aunt Lucrece's part of the castle, but it was like looking in a carnival mirror or at a special effect in a horror film. When she tried blinking, that only made it worse.

Crispin came up beside her. "Do you think we can get back?"

"Sure," said Geena, lying heroically. "How far can it be?"

For once Crispin had nothing to say on the matter. "There's usually a couple lanterns just around the corner. If there's enough kerosene in them, it should give us light until we fall asleep."

"We'll be back with your aunt before that," said Geena, wishing she sounded more certain than she did.

Again Crispin said nothing. He went to get the lamps—the kind she had seen used in westerns—and a box of matches which he called lucifers.

"Here," he said as he lit the first one and adjusted the flame. "Keep it with you all the time, in case we get lost or separated. Don't let go of it."

This order made Geena feel worried, but she took the lamp and watched him light the second one. As she glanced up, she noticed the top of the tower was brilliant with the fading shades of sunset; the sky beyond was turning deep purple-blue. "Let's get going," she said, and prepared to trudge through the old stones that marked the place where walls had stood centuries ago.

"Be careful where you step," Crispin told her. "The ground's uneven."

"So it is," she said. She had nearly bumped her chin on the broken base of a stone column. "I'll be careful. You better do the same." With that she set off in the direction of the other solid part of the castle. It wouldn't take long, she thought. Ten minutes, twenty at the most. It had taken about ten minutes to cross above the ambulatory to the tower. Double that for the gallery, and twenty minutes would see them back with Aunt Lucrece.

They had been walking through the same dull mist in what seemed a straight line for what felt like the greater part of an hour when Crispin signaled a halt. "I have to sit down," he said.

Geena welcomed the opportunity to take break, and looked at once for an outcropping of stone to use for a chair. As she put her basket down, she said, "I didn't think it would take this long."

"I can't see the tower anymore," Crispin observed as he glanced back over his shoulder.

"It's the mist," said Geena, speaking too quickly, for she was beginning to feel frightened again. The place was disorienting, with no sunlight to remind them of direction or time. "It makes it hard to see very far." If only she had noticed some landmarks between the tower and the part of the castle they were seeking, she might be able to keep better track of their progress.

"If there is anything to see," added Crispin for her, as he, too, set his burdens down. He rubbed his hands together and stared around him into the darkness that mixed with the fog. "As long as we've been walking, we might be . . . anywhere."

"Yeah," said Geena reluctantly. "I think I better have a look around." She got up again, and reached for her lantern when she felt Crispin's hand on her arm. In spite of her best intentions, she jumped. "Don't do that."

He let go of her at once. "I don't think it's wise to go off by yourself. It's too easy to get separated. And then I don't know if I could find you again."

"But I won't go far—"

"—you may not think so," Crispin corrected her.

She thought about that before she answered. "Okay. You win. We can sit here for a while and try to get our bearings." She thought it was getting chilly. In a short while, she would be cold. If only she hadn't left her sweater where she tied the boat. Given the way things changed around here, she'd probably never see that sweater again.

"Come on," Crispin urged her. "There's no point to feeling about in the dark. Let's see if we can find somewhere we can wait out the night." He raised his lantern to show that the impenetrable mists were growing denser. Now they were lost in a grey world where only their two lanterns made little forlorn puddles of light on the overgrown rubble around them.

"Where are we going when we start up again? Or were you planning to curl up here for the night?" Geena asked, and quickly explained. "Don't you think we'd better find a

53

place where the ghost usually leaves an open space? I don't want to wake up in the middle of a stone wall, thanks anyway. And from what you've told me about this place, I'm pretty sure that could happen."

"Well, I don't think that could happen," said Crispin, sounding doubtful. "But if it would make you feel better, I'll try to make sure we don't spend the night in a dangerous location. If I can determine what that could be." He gave a crack of laughter. "Not that this isn't dangerous just the way it is." He was trying to behave as if he wasn't frightened, but Geena saw through his bravado.

"Hey, Crispin. We're going to get out of this just fine. We'll be back with your aunt in the morning, and then we can figure out what to do next." She put her lantern a bit nearer to her feet to make the most of the light. "Is it getting darker?"

"Probably," said Crispin fatalistically. "It might all go black, and the lanterns won't do any good at all."

Feeling suddenly tired and defeated, Geena sat down once again. She could feel her muscles grow tight against the cold, and she realized she was very hungry. It didn't seem that long since their meal on the towertop, but once again she was famished. "Do you want something to eat?" she asked, hoping he was hungry, too, so she wouldn't feel so odd about wanting to eat.

"Yes, I do," said Crispin, his voice testy. "But I don't want to go hungry tomorrow. If we don't find our way back—"

"Come on," Geena chided him. "Where could we go? We're inside the castle, even if we can't see it. At least, we *ought* to be inside the castle." As she told him this, she hoped fervently that it was true.

"We could go anywhere," said Crispin. "We don't know where this is, not really. And we don't know what the ghost can do to us. And we don't know beyond any doubt where we actually are." He shrugged. "But why not? If I'm going to starve tomorrow, at least I can eat tonight. And we can finish the wine. It will help you sleep."

54

"I don't know," said Geena dubiously. "Our domestic resources teacher says that it isn't a good thing for kids to
drink." She thought back to the week's project they had done
at the beginning of the semester on substance abuse. With
Marinelle Hunt and Anne Zivnuska and Daphne Pomeroy
she had prepared a demonstration report about drugs and
alcohol. It had made a lot of sense back at Washington High,
but here, in this nowhere place a century ago, her report did
not seem as immediate to her. Especially since there was no
way to get hot water for soup or that spicy herbal tea her
mother often gave her; maybe Crispin was right.

"A child shouldn't drink, of course," Crispin said in that
priggish way of his. "But we aren't children. We're going to
be adults very soon. Why, I have a cousin who is just seven-
teen and has been a married woman for six months. Surely
you don't think she is too young to drink, do you?" He
chuckled.

"She got married at *sixteen?*" Geena demanded, at the
same time remembering what Miz Dunn had said about girls
getting married as young as fourteen in many parts of the
world.

"It was an excellent match," said Crispin smugly as he
made himself comfortable as possible, sitting crossed-legged
on the stones. "Her father arranged the marriage settlement,
and her dowry is large enough that he could afford to find
the best man."

"It sounds like some kind of commercial contract," Geena
said, disgusted at the very idea.

Crispin looked surprised. "Well, of course it is. You
wouldn't want her to enter into a marriage without protection, would you? There are children to consider, as well as
my cousin. And if her husband is fond of her—as he is—
and a man of substance, isn't that better than leaving all to
chance? Only those with nothing can afford to follow their
hearts, as you seem to expect."

"But . . . isn't that important? I mean, what about love?

55

Aren't husbands and wives supposed to love each other?" asked Geena, and was shocked when Crispin laughed.

"That comes with the children," he said, so confidently that she wanted to kick him. "You're not saying that you think a girl should throw herself away on love, are you? Why, what happens when the love is gone? She has no marriage she can depend upon, no binding contract to provide for her children. She is left with nothing. But Odette is protected from such misfortune, thanks to her father's position and wealth. She and her children will want for nothing." He laughed as he saw the dismay on Geena's face.

"That's—" She wanted to say terrible, or disgusting, or awful, but perhaps it was only prudent. She couldn't remember if women at this time in history could even have their own bank accounts. So maybe Crispin had a point. "That's pretty unromantic."

"Marriage is unromantic, to use your phrase," said Crispin with the certainty of a young man who has never doubted his place in the world. "It isn't supposed to be romantic. There are mistresses for such needs, but one doesn't *marry* a mistress. No, in marriage one must be pragmatic, if there is anything of value at stake."

"But surely love and . . . all the rest of it are valuable," protested Geena.

"When there is nothing else to bargain with, I suppose it must be. Only the poor can afford romance. The poor and the bohemian set." He achieved an air of cynicism that he was clearly very proud of.

It bothered Geena to show she was ignorant, but she could not keep from asking, "What bohemian set?"

"Oh, you know. Poets and writers and artists. That lot." He shrugged to show he didn't want to talk about this anymore and opened his basket. "What do you want? I have some pickles left."

"Pickles and sausages—make me one of your sandwiches, please," she said, and pulled out the food remaining in her basket.

"If you'll cut the cheese," he said, as if they were making a truce.

"What about tomorrow?" Geena asked as she set out the last of their food.

"We'll be back at the castle by then," said Crispin, his tone uncertain.

"I hope so. And I hope the ghost left us something to eat there," said Geena with a hard look at their meager fare.

As they set about their meal, Geena was once again troubled. What was happening back home? Had anyone missed her yet? Had anyone searched the museum for her? She thought about dinner at home, and found it suddenly difficult to swallow the sausage. Her mother had been planning on serving swordfish with salsa. Right now that sounded like the best meal in the world, more because her mother was going to serve it to the family at home than because she liked swordfish a lot. But if Geena was missing, would that ruin dinner? Would everyone be too upset to eat? Would they rely on their neighbors for supper while they talked to police and TV news people?

8

They had fallen asleep soon after they finished eating, having little to say to each other that was entertaining, and Geena did not relish another dispute. Now Crispin curled around the base of a broken pillar, and Geena huddled close to the base of a wall. They left one of the lanterns lit, its flame turned down as low as possible, in case they should waken in darkness. The last remaining bits of food had been piled into one basket, the other used to hold the second, extinguished lantern.

The precaution of maintaining some light proved unnecessary, for hours later a diffuse brightness penetrated the haze around them. Geena and Crispin woke as soon as their surroundings lightened. Although they had been very tired, neither had slept very soundly, and both had that frazzled look of poor rest.

"What on earth . . . ?" Geena exclaimed as she caught sight of Crispin.

He rubbed his eyes. "What did you do?" he demanded at the same time.

"Nothing," she said hotly as she stared at him: his hair was different than it had been the night before—a pale ash-blond—and he was now wearing fancier, semimedieval clothing, with silver lacing on a powder-blue doublet, breeches of pale gray velvet, and leggings a pristine white. He might have come out of a '50s swashbuckler movie, one of the big, historical epics where people fenced with broadswords, which Geena knew was wrong. Still, he was very grand to look at, and he matched the quality of the morning. His shoes were the same as yesterday, and his face was unaltered.

"I like your hair better this way," said Crispin.

Geena felt her head and discovered that she now had wavy tresses that hung past her shoulders, a bit redder than before. Her dress, like Crispin's outfit, was changed, too. The waist had dropped to the top of her hips and the neckline was a modified V, heavily embroidered in an elaborate pattern of interlocked keys. The color was a vivid green, like sunshine through summer leaves. She looked down and made a gesture of bafflement.

"The ghost does it," said Crispin, his resignation tinged with pride.

"Well, good for him. Did you put in a request?" Geena countered with no attempt to disguise her annoyance.

"I don't imagine it would make any difference if I did," Crispin said, his momentary satisfaction deserting him.

"How can you be so calm?" Geena was still trying to take it all in. "Don't you know this isn't normal?"

"That's what I've been telling you," he reminded her. He reached over and blew the lantern out.

"Does this happen often?" Geena inquired, trying to sound as unflustered as Crispin.

"Sometimes. Sometimes we stay the same for days and days." He did his best to chuckle. "It could have been a lot worse. We could have been different people altogether."

Now Geena looked dismayed. "Other people?" she repeated, horrified at the thought.

"Yes. You know, someone else." He stared away into the bright fog around them. "It could still turn out that way, I'd wager."

"You mean I wouldn't be *me* anymore? The ghost could make me something else? Someone else?" The enormity of the danger swept over her and left her as breathless as if she had been playing soccer for an hour.

"Of course not," said Crispin, doing his best to sound calm about it.

"But you just said that—" Geena protested.

"I don't know if the ghost can do anything of the sort," he said, unwilling to look her in the eyes.

"This is terrible," said Geena, her voice hushed with fear.

"I doubt it—that it's all that terrible," said Crispin. "Because if you were to become someone else, then that someone wouldn't mind being that someone else. Maybe you were a peasant girl yesterday and the ghost just made you think you came from Washington High and took those classes."

This was so frightening that it made Geena angry. "If the ghost did that, he sure gave me a lot of memories that wouldn't make any sense to a peasant girl a hundred years ago."

"Peasants are ignorant, but not that ignorant," Crispin informed her haughtily. "Unless you think that you have moved a century yourself."

That was an issue Geena had no intention of dealing with now, when there were more immediate problems confronting her. "Has it ever happened to you?" she demanded harshly. She wanted to scream at the sky, to make her protest known before such a calamity could take place, trapping her here forever and unaware that she was missed, and in the wrong time. "And how would you feel if it did?" It was all she could do not to hit him.

"I don't think it ever has. I don't remember anything like that. But if it had, I wouldn't know, would I? So it wouldn't make me feel any way," Crispin answered, still unwilling to look at her.

Geena could not imagine what it would be like to be obliterated, for surely that was what the result of such a transformation would be. She decided she couldn't stand it, and gathered all her resolve. "I won't let it happen."

"The ghost—" Crispin began.

"I won't let it happen," she repeated. "I will continue to be myself for as long as I can breathe. If that ghost is going to get rid of me, he'll have to kill me."

Crispin looked around uneasily. "You don't mean that," he said softly, as if he was afraid they might be overheard.

"You're damn right I do," Geena said, her face shining with determination. She raised her voice to a shout. "You hear that, ghost? If you want to change me into someone else, you'll have to kill me." She hoped she sounded braver than she felt. But she remembered what Miz Davenport had taught them in gym—that if you act as if you can do it, you probably can. If you act as if you can't, then it's impossible. She wasn't going to let the ghost have the advantage, not now.

Crispin looked shocked. He made a swimming motion with one arm as if to push away any lingering presence. "Don't do that."

"Why shouldn't I? Because the ghost might hurt me? He's done all the messing with me he's going to do." She was on her feet now, and pacing the way she saw animals pacing in the zoo. She would never again wonder why they did it.

"Don't shout," Crispin whispered. "Perhaps you don't care what the ghost does, but I do. Let's get back to my aunt before you issue any more challenges, all right?"

"Okay," Geena allowed when she had given his warning a little consideration. "We'd better gather up our things." She looked around for the baskets, and found only the one containing food. The second one, where they had put the unused lantern, was gone. Geena shuddered as she made a last look around the area.

"If we keep going that way," said Crispin, pointing along the line of the fallen pillars, "we should find something eventually. If we don't vanish, like the other basket," he added in a melancholy tone.

"We won't vanish," said Geena with more decision than she actually felt.

"Okay," he said, and started to walk, the lantern in his hand.

Geena picked up the basket—it was much lighter now—and swung it to show her confidence. She heard the clink of jars inside, which reassured her. At least they had some food left, though the idea of pickles with fruit preserves made her feel slightly ill. She refused to be stressed out by their predicament. "It looks brighter up ahead. Maybe the fog's lifting."

"It's possible," said Crispin, though his manner said it wasn't likely.

But after about ten minutes of walking, the mists evaporated, and they found themselves standing on the edge of a moat filled with water lilies, and the gray walls of the castle rising in their midst. Looking at it, Geena hoped it was the same castle she and Crispin had left the afternoon before, and not something conjured up by the ghost in the night.

"How do we get across?" she asked.

"There's bound to be a drawbridge, there always is," said Crispin uncertainly. "If we go around on the shady side, we might find it." He adjusted the doublet he wore, fussing with the frill of silver lace at his wrist. "This could get in the way," he offered as explanation.

"It's . . . very pretty," said Geena, who felt she ought to say something.

"Let's try around this way," he suggested, pointing to the left. "The water lilies aren't so thick in that direction."

Geena wanted to ask why that would make Crispin think that the drawbridge was in that direction, but she didn't want any more arguments with him this morning. So she trudged after him, holding her skirt with her free hand when the ground underfoot became marshy. Her skirt was so full that she ended up with a thick handful of fabric before she was able to keep the material from getting damp. Once again she was missing her jeans. "I wouldn't care if they got a little muddy," she muttered to herself.

Crispin overheard her, and said, "These clothes don't get muddy, or dirty."

"That's another of the ghost's tricks, I suppose?" Geena said, still taking care of her skirt—it would be too easy to trip over if she didn't keep hold of it.

"That it is," said Crispin, sounding pleased. "Not everything he does is bad, you know."

Something that had been bothering Geena tweaked at her mind just then as she picked her way through the soggy grass. "Say, Crispin, why is it you call it a ghost in the singular, and your Aunt Lucrece says ghosts, in the plural? Is there one or more of them?" She realized that she was sounding as if she actually believed this ghost stuff. "Not that any of them are—"

"Real? Can you say that after last night?" He gave her a moment to answer, then went on, "My Aunt Lucrece thinks there are several of them. She can't imagine all those things done by just one. She may be right, but I don't know that ghosts are so limited, so I tend to assume there is only one of them. You've seen for yourself what the ghost—or ghosts—can do. You don't expect me to think your protestations of doubt are genuine, do you?"

Geena regarded him stubbornly before she answered. "Well, I don't know yet. Last night was weird, completely weird, but then, this whole painting is, so . . ." Her words straggled off.

"Painting?" repeated Crispin sarcastically. "That's asking for more credence than believing in a ghost or two. Or are you attempting to find another explanation for what you've experienced, and you want to convince yourself that a painting did it? That's a ludicrous idea." He tossed his now-blond hair. "You are asking more of me than I can reasonably accommodate."

Now Geena felt he was mocking her. "I helped you get out of it."

"After you got me into it," he reminded her. "Neither of us would have been in that part of the castle if you hadn't insisted we go there." He set his jaw to make it clear he held her accountable for everything that had happened to him.

"Well, if you're so worried about the castle, we'd better find that drawbridge and get back to your aunt before something else happens to us." She glanced at the shining east wall of the castle; the morning light making the gray stone glisten. "One ghost or more, the castle is a very strange place."

"You'd do well to keep that in mind," said Crispin bluntly. He was quite handsome in his blue and silver with his fair hair. Geena could not help staring at him. Yesterday she would not have thought he could look this good.

"That green is flattering to you," said Crispin, aware of her scrutiny and returning it. "And your hair is much better that way."

"Does the ghost make these changes often? Clothes and hair and all the rest of it?" Geena asked, still worried that she might cease to exist and be made into someone who would not know about her talent for thinking herself into paintings. *If it is a talent and not a curse,* she added to herself.

"Not every day, no," said Crispin. "Occasionally we may go for as much as a week without any transformation. I recall one month last year when nothing changed. We thought the ghost was gone. But then the west wing disappeared for three days, so we knew it was back. Since then the pattern has been fairly regular in good weather. Generally we change once every three or four days, though there might be color variations during the day. In bad weather, only the interiors change."

"Ghosts don't like rain?" Geena suggested.

"I don't think that rain, or snow, would matter to a ghost. But the countryside is dreary in the rain, and that may be why it doesn't change." He coughed delicately.

"But there are changes inside," Geena mused aloud.

"There are," said Crispin, and looked down at his soaked shoe. *"Sacré nom,"* he swore.

"What kind of changes happen inside when it's raining?" Geena continued, with no sympathy for his accident.

"The rooms . . . it's as if the stones . . . they change color. Sometimes they are so dark they are almost purple, at other times, they glisten like marble." He stopped walking and looked back at her.

"So it changes as the light changes," said Geena. "That's the key to it, isn't it? The angle of the light sets the ghost off."

"Apparently," said Crispin, making a face as his other shoe sunk into a boggy patch.

Geena avoided the place, saying with a touch of doubt, "I can't see a drawbridge yet."

"Nor can I. We'll find it, though. All we have to do is keep looking. It's always around somewhere." He slogged on ahead of her, uncaring at the smirching his clothes took. He did not bother to see if Geena was following him, taking it infuriatingly for granted that she was.

"But what if it isn't today?" Geena persisted, hating herself for being frightened but driven to ask the question.

"It will be," he said, bordering on smugness once again.

Between her skirt and the basket, Geena had all she could deal with as she went after Crispin. Occasionally she glanced around to see if she could locate the boat that had brought her the afternoon before. She would need it when she left, for she had to go out of the painting the same way she entered it.

"Ah!" Crispin cried out, pointing ahead. "There it is. I told you we'd reach it."

Geena would have liked to shade her eyes for a better look, but squinted in order to make out the rough planking that crossed from the bank to the castle stones. "We could go in through the garden," she suggested, just to make him as annoyed with her as she was with him.

"If the garden is there this early in the day," he said, unfazed by her remark. "It usually doesn't appear until noon. Best use the drawbridge. It's what I intend to do."

She gave in. "Lead the way."

As he started toward the bridge, he said, "Be careful as you go."

"Why? Is there quicksand?" She wanted to sound braver than she felt.

"No. But there are snakes, sometimes." He shuddered at the word.

65

"I'm not afraid of snakes," said Geena, pleased that it was true. She had often handled the king snake and the rosy boa in their science lab, and had never found the dry touch of their scales and the muscular strength of their long bodies unpleasant. The only part she didn't like was feeding them live mice. That was pretty gross. But right now she wouldn't mind having to feed mice to the snakes twice a day if it would get her back home again.

"Well, don't step on one, anyway," said Crispin.

They reached the bridge without incident, and crossed it quickly, both of them relieved to be within the stone walls once more.

As they entered the central courtyard, Crispin set his lantern down and called out, "Aunt Lucrece! We're back!" He waited and called out the same thing again.

Finally there came an answer. "Crispin! Oh, thank God you've returned."

9

Like Geena and Crispin, Aunt Lucrece wasn't quite the way she had been the previous afternoon. She leaned over the balustrade of the gallery one story above the courtyard, and for the first time Crispin and Geena had a good view of her. This morning her hair was redder and done up in one of those pillow-like hairdos of a hundred years ago. And her clothes, though still semimedieval were now more revealing—a form-fitting peach-colored garment of a stretchy fabric like jersey with a scooped neck and long full skirt; over this she wore a loose sleeveless surcote of heavy damask silk the color of straw, in the style that was called the gates-of-hell. The soft lethargy which had possessed her the first time Geena had seen her had been replaced with a kind of energy that made Geena think that Aunt Lucrece must be one of those women who ran out of steam in the middle of the day, as her own grandmother did. Or maybe the ghost had changed more than her wardrobe and hairstyle.

Geena tried to convince herself that there was nothing to this change other than appearance, that Aunt Lucrece was no different than if she had gone shopping for a new outfit and had stopped in at the salon for a new cut-and-style. But she could not shake the nagging doubts that filled her. She did her very best to smile. "It was quite a night," she admitted.

"*Saint Denis!* Look at you!" This was followed by a single sigh. "At least you're safe," said Aunt Lucrece as she came rushing down the stairs into the courtyard to embrace Crispin and kiss Geena on both cheeks. "I would have sent someone out to look for you, but there was only my maid, and she won't set foot out of the chapel after dark. She is deluded enough to think the ghosts cannot reach her there." She made a motion suggesting exasperation, then stared directly at Geena. "Are you satisfied now, child?"

"No," Geena heard herself say. "I'm not."

"You're not?" Aunt Lucrece repeated as if Geena had suddenly gone insane. "But when the castle disappeared and only the tower remained, and you were at the mercy of the ghosts, weren't you frightened?"

"Of course I was," said Geena honestly. "But if people only did the things they weren't afraid of, none of us would ever learn to walk, and we'd never have learned to make fire." She gave Crispin a friendly-but-defiant look, her face showing more determination than he had yet seen in her. Now that the worst was over, she was determined to tackle the puzzle once again.

"She's a very stubborn girl," Crispin informed his aunt unnecessarily.

"I'm not stubborn," Geena objected, then said, "Well, maybe I am, but that's not bad, is it?" She swung her arms out, including the whole of the courtyard as she said, "I don't know how else to be in a place like this. I wish I did. There's probably some simple, direct thing I could do that would make the ghost realize what it's doing to all of us. Then we could arrange to stop it."

"Do you suppose it would care? What difference do you think it would make if you did? Why should the ghost pay any attention to what you do?" asked Crispin in the most world-weary voice Geena had ever heard in a kid. His blue-and-silver finery looked tawdry now, as if echoing his sentiments.

"I won't know the answer to that until I give it a try," said Geena, doing her best to keep her waning confidence intact. "And I know that if I *don't* try, I'll never get it out of my head that I could have done something." She started to pace in a manner more appropriate to jeans than long skirts. "It's like when I learned how to do a handstand on the uneven bars. It looked hard and risky, but I wouldn't have been able to stand going back to gym class if I didn't try to do it."

"What are you talking about?" Crispin asked, staring at her with a baffled expression.

"You mean the school, the gymnasium?" said Aunt Lucrece.

"No," answered Geena. "School isn't just for gym. That's only a small part of it," she said.

"According to her," said Crispin in his haughty way, "she goes to a school called Washington High. She studies a number of subjects, none of them would be found in a French gymnasium."

"Why would you want to study anything but P.E. in a gymnasium?" Geena asked, her puzzlement increasing. She ventured a guess to account for their continuing misunderstanding, recalling something from her world events class of two semesters ago. "You mean a whole school when you say gymnasium, don't you? That's what you call a high school here, isn't it? The school where you go when you're through with children's school—when you're my age. And it's everything, classes and labs and all the rest. Not just the physical education part."

"If our gymnasium is the same as your high school," Crispin crossed his arms and directed a look of disapproval at Geena, and he declared, "I wouldn't study anything at your Washington High." He scowled, which did not fit with the look of his pale blue-and-silver clothes, which seemed appropriate only for smiles and laughter.

"Well, you'd have to do more than gym class, that's for certain," Geena told him, refusing to fight with him because she knew he was in the mood to argue.

Sensing something of the discomfort between the two, "What is a gym class? What do you study?" asked Aunt Lucrece.

"Gymnastics, of course," said Geena, then realized neither Crispin nor his aunt understood her. "Tumbling, to begin with, and then work off the floor. I'm trying to build up my routine so I can get into competition." She stopped, remembering she would have to get back in order to continue her gymnastic studies. Her chin lifted as much to defy her predicament as to challenge Crispin and Aunt Lucrece. "I do work on the uneven parallel bars, and some floor patterns." She saw they still did not comprehend. "Physical exercise, with balance and control."

"Ah," said Crispin. "Games."

"Not really," Geena tried to correct him, and had to admit defeat.

"But surely it's nothing strenuous? That can be dangerous, like riding to hounds at the wrong phase of the moon," said Aunt Lucrece, who blushed and then shook her head. "Is it one of those progressive schools, with physical culture instruction? I've read about them, but—"

Geena did her best to think of her school as Aunt Lucrece might. "It would probably seem that way to you," she allowed.

"How American," said Crispin. "You're worse than the English when it comes to games, as though education lay in the muscles and not the mind." He showed his opinion in the slight sneer that touched his upper lip.

"It isn't games, it's fitness," said Geena, aware that this would mean little to either Crispin or Aunt Lucrece. "And it's important." She didn't want to get into an argument about it, not now. "Right now, it doesn't mean much."

"For once we have the same thought," said Crispin, his manner a bit less scornful. "I can just say I am glad I don't have to go to your Washington High School. It sounds like a . . . an inappropriate place for me."

"I'm glad, too," Geena responded with feeling. "You wouldn't like it at all."

Sensing that yet another dispute was about to begin, Aunt Lucrece said, "I think we had better go inside. You must be hungry, and I suppose you might want a bath." She smiled warmly and made a number of gestures to show she wanted everything to go well.

70

Crispin picked up his lantern and the basket, and said, "I'll take these to the kitchen. Is cook about?"

"Yes," said Aunt Lucrece. "There should be pastries waiting for you. I ordered that some be prepared for you, for when you got back."

"Thank you," said Geena, determined to be polite for the time being.

"I'm just grateful you're both back unharmed," said Aunt Lucrece, with a long glance at her nephew. "How could I explain to your mother what became of you?"

That remark brought a rush of anguish to Geena. She was starting to feel very lost, and that worried her. She had to keep her mind on getting back to her time and her place. She did her best to think about home. What was *her* mother doing this morning? Geena wondered. Surely she had called the police by now, and there might have been something on the news about her disappearance. She imagined all her friends had been called, and their families were worried for their kids because she was gone. How could she explain about where she had been when she got back? *If* she got back.

That last possibility made her suddenly unable to swallow, as if there was a pebble caught in her throat. She forced herself to breathe slowly and deeply as she went into the castle with Crispin and his aunt. It was likely she'd feel better after a long bath and something to eat. She was sorry now she hadn't brought a toothbrush and some toothpaste.

The cook was a large, placid woman with a round face, about forty or so, rust-colored hair starting to go gray. Hers was an open face and she had a cozy, plump body enveloped in a white apron. She was up to her wrists in bread dough, and she continued to knead as she was introduced to Geena.

"A pleasure to meet you," said Geena, continuing her politeness.

"And you, though you're a foreigner," said the cook with genial indifference.

"Oh, Benoite, how foolish you are." Crispin chided affec-

71

tionately, adding to Geena, "She thinks anyone living more than a day's walk from here is a foreigner, don't you, Benoite?"

"You can say what you like Monsieur Crispin," Benoite declared, giving the dough a particularly hearty pummeling, "but it is true. Those from farther away than we can walk in a day are always foreign to us. Say what you will, you know it is so. If you cannot reach a place in a day, it is foreign."

Listening to this exchange, Geena wondered what Benoite would think of the jets that could whisk her around the world in a day. Would she then declare that there were no foreigners? Geena doubted it.

"If you insist," said Crispin, losing interest in their dispute as soon as he began it. "When will the bread be done?"

"In two hours, and well you know it," said Benoite. She spread a damp cloth over the bowl of dough and said, "Now let's see about getting the water heated for your bath. The bread needs to rest while it rises."

Preparing the bath turned out to be more complicated than Geena was used to. First, three large buckets were taken to the sink where the pump stood. The buckets were heavy and awkward to handle. Then Crispin worked the pump arm while each of the buckets was filled in turn. They were now quite hard to heft and it was an effort to carry them to the big iron stove and wrestle them onto the surface.

"When they're hot enough, we'll pour them into the tub. You take those thick kitchen mitts to carry the buckets, otherwise you could get burned or scalded." Crispin gestured to a small door on the far side of the kitchen. "You can wash first," he offered, making it clear that this was a major concession on his part.

"Thanks," said Geena, who was feeling grubbier than she liked, as if she had been to the beach and not gotten all the sand off. She decided it was from sleeping on the stones in that lost part of the castle. Sand or dust or some other fine particles had got inside her clothes. She wondered what she ought to do about her hair; perhaps she should borrow scissors and cut it off. But if the ghost didn't like it, what then? She decided to make up her mind about it while she soaked.

While they waited for the water to heat, Crispin and Geena ate flaky rolls filled with spiced ham, and washed them down with apple cider while Benoite fussed about the kitchen, chopping vegetables and churning cream into butter. She was glad they liked her cooking, beaming with satisfaction when Crispin praised the quality of their breakfast.

Geena watched, astonished at how long everything took, and how little that seemed to bother anyone but her. How could she stand to live here one day more, where she felt stifled and restricted? At last she said, "I don't know how you stand working at that pace."

"It is the modern way," said Benoite with a lift of one big shoulder. "I do not mind the rush."

Geena was about to protest Benoite's use of the word *modern* when she was struck again with the thought that this was as modern as these people could be. Each day was as new and uncertain to them as each new day at home was to her. Like Geena in her own time, they did not know how things would turn out. She would have to deal with this past as the present for a while longer if she was to get home safely. She tried to recall what had been done toward the end of the last century. The electric light had been invented, but few places had it. Trains were the major means of long-distance travel. Steam ships crossed the ocean. There was a telegraph, and probably a telephone or two in the major cities. But so many things she took for granted were far ahead of this era. And the people in this time and place did not miss faxes and copiers and televisions and computers. Their time, for them, was modern times—her time was the unanticipatable future. It was not an easy thing to keep in mind.

For a moment the room darkened, as if outside a cloud had passed over the sun.

"The water will be hot in a while," said Benoite placidly.

73

"I will make you an omelette while you wait for the water to heat."

"Good," said Crispin, smiling eagerly for the first time.

Geena knew it was useless to fret. In this time, you waited for the water to heat if you wanted a hot bath. And since she did, she had to resign herself to waiting, like everyone else.

10

She felt better after washing, though handling all that hair in the bath had turned out to be more of a trick than she had anticipated, and she had had a struggle rinsing it. Geena had wanted to get back into her jeans, but Crispin had persuaded her that the ghost might be offended by her actions, and might decide to change her in some way she would like even less. In the end, she had got back into the outfit she had awakened in that morning. Sure enough, it was just as Crispin had said—the clothes were as fresh and clean as if they had just come from the dry cleaner's back home in the 1990s.

"That's better," said Geena to her reflection as she checked herself in the excellent mirror in the antechamber to the great hall. She was positive no such mirrors had existed in medieval times, and she was glad to have a good, even surface to inspect herself in. The dress was sillier than she had thought, and that bothered her as she contemplated her reflection.

"You will need a comb, I think," said Aunt Lucrece when Geena presented herself in the great hall of the castle. "I must have one somewhere that you can use." She hurried off and returned a short while later with a large white comb that she held out to Geena. "This should do."

Geena looked around. "Where's Crispin?" she asked.

"He's about somewhere," said Aunt Lucrece, some of her earlier vagueness returning. "I should think he will be back in an hour or so. That's what he told me, in any case."

Geena studied the comb Aunt Lucrece had given her, fingering the surface with curiosity. "What's it made of?" she

75

asked as she noticed the faint variations of color in the surface.

"Why, ivory, of course, like all good combs," said Aunt Lucrece, her manner unembarrassed. "I wouldn't give you a wooden one."

"You mean ivory from *elephants?*" Geena was shocked. "But they're an endangered species," she said, and realized as she heard herself speak that this would mean nothing to Aunt Lucrece.

"I can't think why they are in danger. They are too big and powerful to have many enemies. Why, the natives live in fear of them, and who can blame them? Africa is filled with them, and so is India," she said. "I do not like your tone of address, young lady."

Geena did her best to deal with the awkwardness she had created. "It's just that ivory isn't used much at home."

"Too costly, no doubt," said Aunt Lucrece, satisfied by this slight explanation. "Well, you may use this one." She smiled at Geena in such a way that Geena felt she had made a fool of herself with her outburst.

As she began to comb her hair, Geena tried not to feel guilty for using the ivory comb. In her own time, she reminded herself, this comb would be an antique, not as dreadful as modern ivory. She was glad to find a tangle to work at, for it gave her a short while to compose her thoughts. Morning was passing quickly, and it would soon be midday. She had so much to do, and there would not be a great deal of time to do it in, not if she was going to get back to her own time this afternoon when, if Crispin and his aunt were right, the moat would be in the same place it was when she crossed it yesterday. She looked around the great hall of the castle, and noticed that the chairs were of the overstuffed and wing-backed nineteenth century sort, not the stark wooden frames of medieval times. There were other touches, too, in the form of a box of cigars as well as a half-dozen framed photographs set out on the sideboard. And the lights in the room were not candles or oil lamps, but gaslights—the kind that had been in her great-grandmother's house. The third snarl of hair proved to be too much for Geena. "I'm not a long-hair kind of girl," she announced out of nowhere. "Do you have scissors?"

"Of course I do," said Aunt Lucrece. "I have embroidery snips and pinking shears for sewing, and paper scissors, and household scissors, for twine and other such." She watched while Geena strove to make her hair cooperate. "You shouldn't cut out tangles like that one," she said by way of minor correction as she observed Geena's struggle. "Your hair will grow unevenly if you do."

"I don't want to cut this out," said Geena calmly, "I want to cut the hair *off*." She paid no heed to the scandalized expression on Aunt Lucrece's face. "I can't stand it this way."

"What do you mean?" she demanded. "Surely you don't intend . . . the ghosts will not approve if you do anything . . . why do you think you had your hair grow in the night, if not because the ghosts did not like the way it was before? It doesn't become you, looking like a boy. You ought to—"

Geena stopped this expostulation with a single shake of her head. "I'm not going to worry about the ghost. Or ghosts. It's my hair. I don't want it this way, I want it cut the way it was before. If the ghost doesn't like it, he can tell me himself." She looked around challengingly, half-hoping to see a gauzy shape materializing in a corner, or to hear a sepulchral voice rumble through the stones. "And I hope he's listening, because I want to talk to him. I want some answers. There are some things we need to settle, he, or they, and I."

"For goodness sake," said Aunt Lucrece, making a hushing motion. "Don't do that. You mustn't attract the ghosts. They could do . . . anything. Don't make them notice you."

"But that's what I'm trying to do," said Geena with great determination. "I don't know what else to do to get the ghost's attention."

"You can't want the attention," said Aunt Lucrece. "It isn't sensible to want the ghosts' attention." She looked upset at the very idea, and glanced around uneasily as if she feared they were overheard. "You don't know what the ghosts can do."

"Then the ghost, or ghosts, and I are even." Geena smiled, wanting to reassure Aunt Lucrece, as she set the ivory comb aside. "If you'll tell me where I can find the scissors, I'll take care of the rest."

Now Aunt Lucrece was becoming distraught. She put her long, slender hands up to her hair and shook her head as if to clear it. "I cannot believe how foolish you are being."

"Maybe I am being foolish," Geena said, trying to placate the woman who had, by default, become her hostess. "But I won't be treated like a pawn. It's not acceptable to me."

"You must be joking," Aunt Lucrece decided, her assertion giving her a sense of satisfaction and vindication that she was certain would make her point with this young, foreign upstart. "I cannot think you would be reckless enough to do anything so . . . lacking in good sense."

"But it has nothing to do with good sense," Geena persisted. "I don't like my hair this way. I want it back the way it was. So I'm going to do something about it. It's my hair, after all." She knew she was not getting through to Aunt Lucrece but she could not keep herself from continuing. "I'll need those scissors." She would worry about how to explain what had become of her hair when she got back to her own time and place. Right now all that mattered was getting the scissors. She ran her fingers down the cascade of shining tresses. "This is really pretty. Don't get me wrong. But it isn't right for me, that's all."

"You can't want your hair like a boy's," Aunt Lucrece insisted. "You must see it won't do."

Geena realized now that she had gone too far, and that Aunt Lucrece was really upset. She did her best to give a compliant smile, as if the notion to cut her hair was as much Aunt Lucrece's as her own. "I don't think anyone here cares about how I cut my hair, not really. Maybe not even the ghost."

"Then it isn't necessary for you to do it," said Aunt Lucrece as if trying to make her point with Geena. "Please. Consider. You can leave your hair as it is. So pretty and . . ."

"Feminine?" Geena suggested sweetly. "Maybe it is, but it gets tangled and I don't like it," she insisted. "Some girls like long hair. I don't. I want it off."

"Oh, dear," said Aunt Lucrece, her tone becoming ill-used. "I suppose I had best fetch the scissors then, or I suppose you'll find a way to do it with a knife."

"I might gnaw it short," Geena said, enjoying herself and at the same time upset that she did. She attempted an apology. "I didn't mean anything by that, really. It's just that I—"

"You're determined to cut your hair. You've made that plain. And I wash my hands of what might become of you if you do." Aunt Lucrece sniffed and raised her head as she left Geena to herself.

"Fine," said Gena. While Aunt Lucrece was out of the room, she busied herself going from one elaborate wood carving to another—each pillar holding up the gallery was a mass of sculpture. She hadn't noticed before. Perhaps, the thought intruded, the carvings were something new, a recent change that had been made while she was trying to comb her hair and was not paying attention to her surroundings.

Again there was a slight darkening of the light. Geena glanced toward the windows but saw no clouds in the sky beyond. She gave her attention back to the column.

One of the pillars, she noticed, had a number of human figures twining their way up toward the gallery as if caught in a cyclone. Faces and limbs were distorted in the spiraling force the column suggested. She studied it, fascinated and slightly repelled, the way she sometimes felt when she was sneaking a look at her parents' special videos, the ones with the single X rating.

Aunt Lucrece came back while Geena was still puzzling over the pillar. She held out a large pair of scissors with an expression of distaste. "I wish you would not do this," she

79

said, and then clicked her tongue in disapproval when she saw what Geena was looking at.

"What's this supposed to be?" Geena asked, blushing in spite of her determination not to.

"It's the Whirlwind of Lovers. In the *Inferno*, if I remember correctly," said Aunt Lucrece, welcoming this distraction.

"What *Inferno*?" Geena asked, still engrossed in the pillar.

"Why, Dante's, of course. Don't they teach you about great poetry in your Washington High?" Her sarcasm was not as sharp as Geena expected it to be, and that put her on the alert.

"There's a lot of subjects for us to study." She wanted to say that she had to learn things that Aunt Lucrece wouldn't believe were possible, such as operating a computer and taking proper care of a microwave oven. "I don't think we've gotten around to Dante yet." She recalled her mother saying something about the lack of classics in the reading list; it seemed likely that this was one of them.

"Yes," said Aunt Lucrece, her critical attitude returning. "Well, I can understand why the school might not want well-reared girls to read certain portions of Dante, though those might be left out." She extended the scissors a second time. "You said you wanted these. And against my better judgment, I am supplying them."

Geena took the scissors. "Thank you . . . Aunt Lucrece," she said, realizing she had no other name to use for the woman.

"It is hardly worth mentioning," said Aunt Lucrece. "In fact, I hope you will say nothing about my part in this if the ghosts take it in bad part."

"Don't worry. I'll make sure you're off the hook," Geena promised, then went back to the antechamber to make use of the mirror while she chopped her hair off to a length she thought she could stand, letting the lavish strands fall to the floor in a shining heap. She thought the day might come when she would regret doing this, but just now, it felt marvelous to be rid of the stuff.

11

"You look terrible," Crispin announced as he caught sight of Geena. "It looks as if you've used hedge-clippers on yourself." He was slightly altered again, his blue doublet now faded almost to white, and his hair lightened to a silvery-blond color. His practical, 1890s shoes looked woefully out of place with his medieval-like finery.

"Not hedge-clippers," said Aunt Lucrece in her overly patient way which was intended to show her disapproval. "Just scissors. You would have thought she was scything hay."

"Well, I like it," said Geena defiantly, though she was stretching the truth. She knew the ends were all uneven, and that the length of the left side was not quite the same as the length of the right. She had seen cuts that were uneven that looked really good, but she had to admit hers was clearly a mistake; she could not kid herself about that. Her attempts at shaping the cut with the kind of layering she had seen the hairdresser do had not succeeded, though she'd done her best to make the same moves, and hold the hair just so, between her fingers as she cut. When the hairdresser did it, it seemed easy, but she had discovered this was deceptive. To her own eyes, her hair looked like a worn-out pom-pom. But it was better than it had been, and it might be enough to make the ghost do something.

Crispin cocked his fair head and studied her. "You're an obstinate girl, Geena. Mind you don't get yourself into trouble on account of it."

"I'll keep your advice in mind," she said, and asked the question that had been nagging at her for the last half hour. "You've had a look around the castle. What's it like now?"

"A part of the ambulatory is back, and a portion of the

gallery. They'll probably connect up by noon," said Crispin as if this were the most obvious thing in the world.

"And if they don't, what then?" Geena demanded, beginning to be afraid.

"Then it will be difficult to reach the tower, if you want to go back there," said Crispin.

"Why should I want to do that?" Geena asked, more curious than affronted.

"I don't know. But you do seem to want to do any number of nonsensical things that I can hardly anticipate what you may think of next." He grinned at her as if he was satisfied he had won that round.

She decided to take him seriously. Her eyes glistened with determination. "You may be right—if the ghost won't come to me, I'll probably have to go to him. Or her. Or it. Or them." Each additional phrase came out strangely and she did not like the way she felt at the prospect of being back in that peculiar non-place again. She was determined to put a good face on things, however, and tried to smile with confidence. Like her hair, her smile was lopsided.

Aunt Lucrece said something to Crispin in a low voice, very rapidly and in French. Then she favored Geena with a kindly look. "It would be very dangerous to tempt the ghosts to pursue you. For one thing, we would not be able to help you if you were transformed. For another, we cannot anticipate what the ghosts might do if you provoke them. I have told you this, and you continue to ignore my warnings to you. I can only think you are . . . not steady in your mind."

Geena wanted very much to protest this accusation, but she knew it would be foolish to give either Crispin or his aunt any reason to think they were right about her state of mind. "I'm sure what you say is true, but if I don't do this, I may never be able to get back to my family." She had almost said *my own time* but had been able to stop herself before the words were out.

At once Aunt Lucrece's face filled with sympathy and she hurried toward Geena, her arms open to hug her. "You poor

82

child. Of *course* you must want to return to your family. How thoughtless of me to have . . ." She kissed Geena on both cheeks in the French manner. "Your dear mother must be quite beside herself to have you missing."

It was an effort for Geena not to cry. Her eyes brimmed and she tried to turn away from Aunt Lucrece's effusive concern. "I . . . I'm worried about her, and my father, and my brother." She knuckled her tears away and did her best to banish the image of her mother seated at the dining room table, her face with that horrible blank look it had the day her father had died. Geena would never forget that stricken stare. And she was determined not to be the cause of it. She couldn't stand to think that her mother would look like that over her.

"Are they staying near here?" Crispin asked. "Is there some place we could send a message?"

"Don't I wish?" she said, trying to be calm about her predicament. Then she gave a more useful answer. "No, I don't think you can get them a message. I would have suggested it before now if I thought it would work."

"You don't know where they are?" asked Aunt Lucrece in some distress.

"Oh, I know that," said Geena at once, and added, thinking of the gulf of years as well as distance. "I just don't know how to reach them."

"Well, so long as you know their location, Benoite's nephew can take a letter for you, if you know where they are. Or he can post it for you if the distance is great," offered Aunt Lucrece as if such an opportunity might spur Geena to remember. "They must have arrived in the district only recently, for there have been no rumors of Americans in the neighborhood." She looked narrowly at Geena. "You haven't run away, have you? Or been cast off?"

Geena felt color mount in her face, making her skin seem feverish. "No. I didn't run away. And no, I haven't been cast off. But I've . . . gone too far from them." As she defended herself, she was struck by the thought that there had been runaways in this time, too. All those stories about fourteen-year-olds coming to the New World was not just a myth. "I . . . I just went beyond the water lilies. I didn't know it would be so hard to get back from here. It didn't seem dangerous when I first began."

"She came across the moat, remember, in the early afternoon." Crispin had a less superior manner now as he studied Geena's face.

"Yes. *That* moat," said Aunt Lucrece with a significant nod. She rounded on Geena once more, ready to embrace her a second time.

"Whatever that means," Geena added, doing her best to avoid another pair of kisses. "And I have to get back across it to be where I started out." She swallowed hard. "I can find my way once I get back across the moat."

"In a strange country?" asked Crispin skeptically.

"When I'm across the moat, it won't be strange," said Geena and hoped to the tips of her toes it was true.

"Possibly not," allowed Aunt Lucrece, "but perhaps you should take someone with you, in case you are unable to find your way."

"I . . . I don't think that would be a very good idea," said Geena, trying to come up with some explanation for her hesitation to accept help.

But Aunt Lucrece nodded once emphatically. "I take your point. You have no wish to appear compromised."

"Compromised?" Geena repeated, uncertain of her meaning.

"Well," she said with an elegant shrug of her rounded shoulders, "I could not take you—that would not be at all proper. And to have Crispin escort you is unthinkable. So I must concede that in this instance your reticence is well-founded, though it is hazardous for you." She turned to her nephew, her mind made up. "She will have to go alone. Nothing else will suit."

Crispin folded his arms in a disapproving way. "We can't have her racketing about the countryside, Aunt Lucrece. It would be very wrong of her to do it. And as for compromising, that may have already been done, after we spent the night in the same place." He carefully avoided looking at Geena, giving her no opportunity to object.

"Ah, but you were under my roof, and so you were chaperoned," Aunt Lucrece said knowingly. "Once away from these walls, that is no longer the case."

Geena wanted to shout at them both, to tell them that this worrying about chaperons was foolish. The last thing in the world she was worried about was having someone babysit her because she might get a reputation for being a wild girl. But she knew Crispin and his aunt would not understand. She kept silent.

"But Aunt Lucrece, there could be risks to her. Think of the stories we hear every day. To permit a young woman to go about unattended—the countryside is not always hospitable," Crispin protested.

"If there is truly countryside at the other end of that moat," said Aunt Lucrece with heavy significance, something like one of the women in the soap operas Geena's next-door neighbor watched so religiously. Geena half-expected to hear an eerie chord on an organ.

That is another thing that is not around in this place, and time—all kinds of entertainment, Geena thought. And very little advertising. Until now she hadn't realized how much she would miss it. Geena was about to ask a question when Crispin cut into her thoughts.

"Do you remember what is on the other side of the moat at that time of day? I don't." He looked puzzled but not much troubled by this realization. He stared down at his feet and sighed. "One day I would like to find out." He regarded Geena with a combination of envy and respect. "I wouldn't cross the moat. Not at that time of day. So I fear you will have to go alone, little though you may like it. I don't think I'm . . . ready to make the attempt."

Geena had the strong impression he had planned to say something more self-condemning and had changed his mind. She could understand why he would feel that way. Was it possible, she wondered, for Crispin to think himself *out* of a painting as she had thought herself *in*? "All of this isn't getting me through the water lilies," she said, not wanting to become tangled in another wrangle with Crispin and his aunt.

"Perhaps not," said Aunt Lucrece. "But given the risks, are you certain you want to go?"

"Yes," said Geena directly and simply. "I have to."

Aunt Lucrece thought this over, and at last went back to Crispin's side. "Yes. In your position I might feel the same way. You do not want to be separated from your family."

"And all the rest," added Geena, careful not to describe how vast all the rest was. She ran her fingers through her chopped-short hair and shook her head, trying to distract herself from the sudden pang of loneliness that had seized her without being obvious about it.

"Well, then, we should find a way to help you," said Aunt Lucrece, a trifle too brightly. She looked about quickly as if she feared being overheard. "I don't want you to think badly of me, but if you are intending to confront the ghost, could you do it in another part of the castle?" Her face was apologetic. "I don't want you to think ill of me, either, but this is where I live, child, and unlike you, there is nowhere I can go to escape the ghosts. I will have to live with them whether you succeed or not. It's been difficult enough having parts of the building appear and disappear willy-nilly. Now you are proposing to make an issue of it all, and while I can see your point—in your place, I would hope I would have the strength of character to do the same thing—I must ask you to attempt your encounter outside this part of the castle." She had been fiddling with the opening of her surcote, pleating it between her fingers. With an effort she made herself stop.

Geena nodded, feeling chagrined. She had brought such dismay into the woman's life, and the disruption might remain long after Geena was back home. Surely she had some responsibility to Crispin and his aunt to keep them from having more trouble because of her. She nodded. "I'll do what I can. Maybe I can try to reach the ghost outside." The offer was only half-serious, and she made it with a slight smile. "The topiary garden might be a good place."

Crispin shook his head. "I don't think so. It's . . . not the way it was when you arrived." He stared away from her, apparently fascinated by the ornamental carvings that had held Geena's attention earlier.

"Don't tell me the maze is back?" exclaimed Aunt Lucrece, her face actually turning pale.

"I'm afraid so," said Crispin heavily, his face growing somber. "I saw it earlier when I was looking about the castle."

Aunt Lucrece put her hands to her face. "What are we to do?"

Crispin stared at a spot some four feet beyond the stone walls. "There isn't anything we can do," he reminded her, his words sounding like a pronouncement of doom. "The maze is back, and there's an end to it." He made an impatient gesture with his hands. "You don't expect me to dig it up, do you?"

"Heaven forfend," said Aunt Lucrece. She laid her hand on Crispin's shoulder as if to warn and protect him at once. "Don't go near it."

Geena was not only puzzled, she was fascinated. What, she wondered, was it about this maze that terrified Aunt Lucrece and Crispin so much? She tried to recall the topiary garden as she had seen it upon her arrival. There had been a cat, she remembered, and a rooster, and a number of other animals, all clipped from boxwood hedges. She had liked the garden, and hoped it was not gone forever.

"I won't," Crispin assured his aunt with feeling. "I don't want any part of the filthy place."

Aunt Lucrece squared her shoulders. "I had best go warn Benoite," she said, and at once started off in the direction of the kitchen, leaving Crispin and Geena alone.

12

"So why is this maze such a bad thing?" Geena asked Crispin as soon as Aunt Lucrece's footsteps had faded to echoes in the hall. "It's just a bunch of plants. What can it *do?*"

"Do?" Crispin repeated, as if he did not understand her.

"Yes, do. It can't get up and chase you, can it? It can't throw stones at you. It's not so dangerous. The plants it's made of aren't carnivorous, are they?" She had meant this to amuse him so that he would tell her more. The ploy failed.

He refused to answer her directly. "I don't want to talk about the place. It's not good to mention it."

"Why not? Why is the maze any different than the tower? Or the ambulatory? Tell me what you mean, Crispin." She put her hands on her hips, feeling a bit startled to realize that people actually did that when they were upset, or at least she did. "You tell me, or I'll go right now and find out for myself."

He put up a hand in a gesture to stop her. "I don't think you want to do that. It isn't safe."

"What is, in this place?" she asked, flinging out her hand. "Whole sections of this castle come and go like . . . like planets on *Star Trek*." Let him try to figure that one out, she thought triumphantly.

But he was not taking her challenge to heart. "Be sensible, which you say you are, and stay out of the maze. You'll spare yourself grief if you do." He took a couple steps back from her as if to demonstrate that she was on her own.

"Okay," she said decisively. "If you won't tell me I'll find out for myself." It was probably a reckless thing to do, she realized, but she could not stand the humiliation of backing down. She looked directly at him. "You can come with me, or you can stay here."

"You . . . get lost in the maze. Not lost the way you would in most mazes, but lost the way we were last night. Only worse. There are people who have gone into the maze and have not come out again. And that's not just a rumor." He looked defeated now, and with it came a shadow of age, as if losing this fight had leeched all the youth from him.

"You're certain about that? They don't come out somewhere else? I mean, given this place, they could come out anywhere, couldn't they?" In spite of her intense convictions she could not stop being afraid. The only thing more frightening than what Crispin was describing was her growing dread of being stranded in this place forever. That alone spurred her to saying, "Well, if the maze is like that, I'd better give it a try. I could end up somewhere else, and that somewhere else might be the place I'm looking for."

Crispin shook his head. "I'll show it to you. But I won't come with you. Not into the maze."

"Okay," she said, less confidently than she wanted to.

"And I wish you wouldn't go," he told her impulsively. "It's one thing to go back across the moat—when it's in the right place—and another thing to go into the maze. I . . . I think it might make you vanish. Altogether."

Geena squared her shoulders. "I won't know until I try."

"That could be too late," said Crispin quietly, then shrugged. "But if you're determined, who's to say you're wrong?"

She made herself smile at him, though it took more of an effort than she thought it would. "I won't do anything foolish," she assured him.

"Going into the maze is foolish," he said, his voice turning glum as he led the way toward the kitchens and the place where the topiary garden had been the day before and where now there was the fountain and a maze.

It was bigger—much bigger—than Geena had anticipated, the greenery so vast that the well-trimmed walls looked like a carefully groomed forest had made its way up to the door. The hedges were thick, as if they had been planted many, many years ago, and the shape they took was impossible to determine from outside, for the maze towered a good two stories into the air. The opening was near the garden fountain—the same fountain she had sat beside upon her arrival here yesterday; there was a sundial in its center, and Geena calculated the time as eleven-twenty.

"The maze," Crispin announced, as if expecting trumpets to sound.

"I don't think I've ever seen anything like this," Geena admitted just above a whisper as she stared at the impressive outer wall of the maze. She had been in a maze once, one made out of plywood, set up as part of a carnival, and no larger than her grandmother's back yard. This was nothing like that had been, for this one covered far more space and seemed much more threatening.

"It's supposed to cover three acres," said Crispin unhappily.

"I'm not too good at acres," said Geena, who, like most city-raised kids thought in blocks instead of acres. "But it is big." Bigger than the whole of Washington High, including the buildings and the track. She continued to stare, wondering how she would find her way in it. She had thought it would be like figuring her way through a course on Washington High's track, which was a quarter-mile around. But this was a lot bigger than that, and she realized she would have to approach it carefully. She looked at the tall walls of green and said, "Do you have lengths of ribbon I could take with me? In color?"

Crispin shook his head, not indicating he didn't have the ribbon, but in disbelief at the question. "Why would you want it?"

"To tie to the bushes, of course, to mark where I've been, and what turns I've made. I will need four colors. One for the way I've come in case I have to find my way back, one for a way I've tried that turns out to be a dead end, one for

90

anything that changes while I'm in the maze, and one to
mark the entrance and exit. So. Four colors. Maybe red,
blue, yellow, and white. Green won't do much good. And not
brown or anything too dark, like purple." She felt proud of
herself, coming up with such a good idea, and so quickly,
too.

"Four colors of ribbon. I'll ask my aunt. Anything else?"
He was not as sarcastic as he had been.

"Something to eat. This could take a while, and I don't
want to get too hungry." She did her best to sound jaunty,
but inside she felt her nerves twangle like out-of-tune strings.
The only thing that kept her from bolting back into the castle
was pride. She would not let Crispin see her afraid.

"All right. It shouldn't take me long," he said as he turned
on his heel and went back into the kitchen door.

Geena took advantage of the time to walk along the curving wall of the maze. She wanted to get some idea of its size
and the completeness of it. Give how quickly it had appeared, the ghost might have left some of it unfinished, like
those gray nothing places she had experience yesterday. She
had to be ready for more of the same. If she had some idea
where those nonplaces might be, she could try to avoid
them, or prepare for them. Assuming she could see them
coming. That thought brought her up short. The grayness
could come quickly, and if she had no warning she would
not be able to protect herself from it. Again she wished she
had her jeans on, as much for their familiarity as for their
usefulness. It would be easier to think about getting back
home in jeans than in this dress.

A short way along the curve of the outside hedge of the
maze a ladder leaned against the greenery. *Probably for a
gardener,* thought Geena, *someone who prunes the hedges into
shape.* She looked around, and when she found no one, she
went to the ladder, gathered up her skirts and climbed carefully upward.

As she reached the top, she could barely see over the
hedge, and all she could make out was a vast expanse of

green, broken here and there by shadowed areas Geena took to be the paths inside. If she could have a look at the way the maze was laid out, it could make her whole search easier. But she couldn't tell for sure if the dark areas were paths, or only places where the hedges needed more pruning. It was very frustrating. Had someone been holding the ladder for her, she would have taken a chance and climbed to the next-to-the-last rung. But by herself, and in long skirts at that, she thought it was too dangerous, and, after waiting for Crispin for a short while, she climbed down again, taking care to hold her skirt out of the way of her feet.

By the time she was back on the ground, Crispin was coming toward her carrying a canvas bag over his shoulder. "You shouldn't have done that," he said critically.

"Would you have done it for me?" she asked, not wanting to argue.

He thought it over. "No."

"Why? Doesn't the ghost like it?" She had intended this to sting.

Clearly it did. "It's not the ghost. It's not safe for you to climb ladders like that, ghost or no ghost." He offered her the canvas sack. "Here. Food, water, and three colors of ribbon. Cut into ten-inch lengths. It's all Aunt Lucrece could spare." He looked a bit apologetic as she took it from him. "I'm sorry I can't go with you, but . . . well, you know."

"I think I do," Geena said in answer. "This is where you live and you don't want to leave it."

"Yes," said Crispin, the scowl fading from his face. "That's exactly it."

"Then you should know why I have to do this," said Geena very directly. "I want to get to where I live. And it isn't here."

"Washington High," said Crispin with a lopsided smile.

"Yeah. Washington High." She slung the handles of the sack over her shoulder, and with more courage than she actually felt, she started toward the entrance to the maze.

13

Two steps into the maze and the hedge curved around to the left so that Geena lost sight of the fountain at once, and the musical sound of its splash was replaced by the soft whispering of the small leaves of the hedges. The sun, while fairly high in the sky, was still not directly overhead, as it would have been farther south. As a result, the paths were still partially in shadow, sunlight a sharp, bright edge about a third of the way up the inner walls of the maze. She stopped to tie a rust-colored ribbon to the nearest boxwood branch she could reach in the dense wall of green. She had to be right next to the outer wall, she thought. The castle garden was on the other side of the hedge, she was sure of it. She had not gone far enough to be anywhere else. The niggling sense that this consideration had made no difference when she and Crispin had tried to get from the tower to the castle did nothing to improve her sense of accomplishment.

Nine steps further on and the maze branched. One path led to the left again, and then to a T-junction she could just see. The other led around to the right, doubling back on the way she had come. In almost all the maze puzzles she had ever done, the doubling back was the right choice so she decided to go to the left, to the T-junction, and to choose then which way to go. She tied another rust-colored ribbon to the entrance to the T-junction, and could not help but look back at the first ribbon she had tied. She was shocked at how important it was to her to see that first ribbon.

She thought she heard Crispin calling her name, but the constant susurrus of the leaves made too much noise for her to be sure. "Probably wishful thinking," she said aloud, for the satisfaction of hearing a human voice, if only her own. The sound of it was small against the persistent sound from the hedges, almost, thought Geena, as if the plants were whispering about her.

The T-junction offered another left or right choice, and this time she chose right, marking the choice with yet another ribbon. The path ran in a long curve for quite a distance, and Geena found herself walking very quickly, as if trying to find another intersection of paths. Finally, after walking for what felt like the length of two city blocks, the path she was on took an abrupt turn to the right into a kind of traffic circle where five paths converged. Looking at the angle of sunlight on the walls of the maze, Geena realized she had turned more than ninety degrees from where she had started out, and that unnerved her. She also saw that the day was advancing and she would soon be in direct sunlight, which she hoped would make her task easier. As it was, she had now to choose which of these four additional paths she ought to take. She decided against the leftmost, reasoning it had to end somewhere between the outer wall and the long curving path she had just come down. The second left-hand one might be more promising, but she feared it might also stay in the outer reaches of the maze and she wanted to get to the center.

As she tied another ribbon to the entrance to the path she had come on, she tried to get her bearings. "Yeah. Right," she said aloud, aware that the purpose of a maze was to disorient. To keep from worrying about her predicament, and from becoming jittery, she thought about the word disorient: *dis*, not or against. *Orient*, the east. To not know which way is east, hence to lose one's sense of direction. She could hear prissy, frog-faced Mister Shelby explaining it in her head, as he had last year in English composition class. She had hated it then and missed it now almost as much as she missed french fries and CDs.

For several minutes she debated between the two right-hand paths, and finally chose the one to the far right. She tied another ribbon to the entrance to that path and set out along it, trying to keep an eye on the angle of the light so that she would not be disoriented again.

The path ended in a blunt dead end, and for a moment Geena fought the sudden onslaught of fear that this place was a prison and she had been foolish enough to enter it of her own free will. Then she turned around and trudged back the way she came, returning to the five-way intersection in a short while. She untied her first ribbon and replaced it with a pale blue one, to indicate the path was false. The rust-colored ribbon she kept in her hand to use on the next way she tried.

She put her hands on her hips and glared at the many pathways. "All right. I came down that one, and I've checked out this one. Let's try the next one over. Might as well be methodical. That's what they always tell us in math class." She fixed the rust-colored ribbon to the entrance to the path and gave it a playful tweak. "Here goes nothing."

With determination she gathered up her skirts again and set off. She wondered as she walked if she ought to be talking to herself—wasn't that what crazy people did? Crazy people talked to themselves. "But," she said, trying to be lighthearted, "think about it—you're off adventuring in a painting, chasing a ghost in a maze that comes and goes like a special effect. Go ahead. Talk." She was able to chuckle at herself.

The second path she tried proved to be what she had been looking for, its path leading a dizzying journey through turns, reverses, curlicues, arabesques, and Greek keys. It wound its way far around to what Geena supposed was the far side of the maze.

This time there were six paths to choose from.

Geena made a gesture of exasperation. "Great!" she shouted at the maze. "Just great! And I bet the next junction—when I find it—has seven choices. Who laid out this thing, anyway?" If the ghost had appeared at that moment she would have yelled at it for creating such a complex mess for her to deal with. "Okay," she said as she forced herself to think reasonably. "The middle path is too obvious. And the second from the right is too easy, too, so I'll start out with the second on the left." With that she marched up, tied a rust-colored ribbon to a boxwood branch and set out.

The pathway turned sharply twice and dead-ended at a statue of a centaur. Undaunted, Geena retraced her steps and tried again.

Forty minutes later, three pale blue ribbons marked the entrances to the paths she had tried. She stood at the six-way junction and glowered at the various untried paths to cover the sinking feeling that was taking hold of her. "Maybe," she said quietly, "maybe the center is so obvious it isn't obvious at all. Maybe the center is the way to go, because everyone will stay away from it because it is the center." She rubbed her hair and tried to muster her confidence for another attempt at the maze. She tied a rust-colored ribbon to the entrance to the center pathway, adjusted the bag over her shoulder, and recommenced walking.

After walking for a considerable distance—she estimated it was about two long blocks—along a curving path, she decided she must have chosen the right one, for all the wrong selections had ended fairly shortly, and this one seemed to continue endlessly, like some strange background loop in a cheap cartoon. Things were definitely looking up. Had the whisper of the leaves been quieter, she might have whistled.

An unwelcome notion intruded on her self-approval: what if the ghost had changed the maze since she entered it? What if the center of the maze had been moved, and would continue to move so that she could walk all day and into the night without finding it? She really didn't know that much about the ghost. Would it be amused by her plight? All at once she thought she could get very hungry during her exploration of the place.

"At least I can follow the ribbons out," Geena told herself, hoping to encourage herself once again. "It's not as if I'm stuck in here forever." Now that she had gone a fair distance, the sack over her shoulder was getting heavy.

The raucous caw of a crow disrupted her thoughts. She looked up sharply and saw the large, black bird perched at the top of the maze. It cawed again, the sound reminding Geena of the sound a squashed bagpipe might make. Hadn't she read somewhere—probably in Mister Shelby's class—that a group of crows was called a murder? She wished she had something to scare it away. It reminded her of Van Gogh's last painting, of crows flying over a field of wheat. It was the painting he did before he shot himself.

With a third, louder cry, the crow spread its big, black wings and flew away. Geena watched it go, feeling a relief she could not explain.

"It's just a bird, a bird with a really rotten voice," she said to the long, curving, green corridor. "If someone were with me, I wouldn't pay any attention." That much she was fairly sure was true. If her friends were here, the crow would not mean anything. If her friends were here, going down this long path hemmed in by neat hedges would be a lot more fun than it was alone. "Of course," she reassured herself, "it would take a lot longer because we'd end up arguing about which way to go." At the moment that didn't seem to be such a bad trade-off.

The next junction brought three paths together, and the center of their convergence was marked by a statue of a faun playing pipes. Looking at the statue, Geena noticed the faun had a strong resemblance to Crispin, if Crispin had had a short curly beard, cloven feet, and short, curly horns.

She walked around the statue several times, then said, addressing her question upward, "Is this supposed to mean something?"

When no answer came—not that she expected one—she made a quick motion with her hand as if to push something unpleasant away. "Okay, okay," she said in response to her inner urgings. Impulsively she chose the path that the faun was not facing, and after putting another rust-colored ribbon in place, went on. This time the dead end took about ten minutes to reach, and was made less imposing by an old crabapple tree with a bench beneath it. After a moment, she flung herself down on it, and opened the sack. "Might as well have lunch," she said aloud.

Crispin had packed the bag with an assortment of things, including three hard-boiled eggs; hard, spicy sausages; a small pot of brownish mustard; two kinds of cheese, one with a soft, smelly rind; a jar of mixed pickles; a small pot of butter; two fresh carrots and half a dozen fresh radishes; four soft rolls; thin slices of smoked ham; a softened glob of paper-wrapped chocolate; a knife, fork, spoon, and napkin; a bottle each of water and wine; and three green apples.

Looking at this laid out in front of her on the bench, Geena was ravenous. She began with an egg, throwing the shell near the base of the tree in the hope it would be good for it; her mother was always putting things like eggshells out in their small garden.

Next it was the pickles—puckery, sour-sweet peppers, olives, beets, something crunchy and greenish-white she'd never seen before, and little cucumbers. Their tang was delicious, and she stopped when she had eaten a third of them, though she wanted to finish off the jar. The sensible thing, she knew, was to eat the vegetables while they were still fresh, but she really wanted some of the cheese, in a sandwich with butter. Only the prospect of having to spend the night in this bizarre place made her obey the promptings of her logic instead of the whim of her hunger, and settle for the carrots, with an apple for dessert. She figured the radishes would keep a little longer—they always did in salads.

She drank about half the water and would have had more, but she did not want to run out, so she capped the bottle and put it back in the sack with the rest and made herself go back to the faun, taking off the rust-colored ribbon from the entry to the path she had just tried and replacing it with a light blue one.

Maybe the faun was an indicator. She glanced down the avenue the statue faced, noticing that it made an abrupt turn early on. Since it was that one or go back the way she came, she did the logical thing, put a rust-colored ribbon on the hedge and started away from the faun once again.

14

Geena had not gone more than a hundred yards along the new path when she once again came upon a crabapple tree with a bench beneath it, though this time three other paths converged there. She marked the way she had come with a rust-colored ribbon, noting she had only six left. Then she flung up her free arm and said, "Real funny," to the tree, and approached it reluctantly. Carefully she looked around its base and was relieved that she found no eggshells there.

The leaves of the tree rustled, though there was no increase in wind that Geena could feel. A grue slid up her spine as she watched the tree shake in a nonexistent tempest. Half a dozen apples dropped from its branches as the tree continued to bend and shake. None of the boxwood hedges moved, though the whisper of their leaves grew louder. It was as if a very small tornado had landed in this little open space in the middle of the maze.

"Okay. Enough!" Geena shouted as she watched the tree. "You want something, ghost, you come and tell me yourself. No more *Twilight Zone*. No more showing off. Cut this weird—"

A crow came flapping down to land in the crabapple tree. It clung tenaciously to an upper branch as the tree bent and flailed. It fixed Geena with its shiny eye and cawed twice.

Geena clapped loudly and made the hooting noise that once made Louise Potter put her hands over her ears and hunch down into her shoulders.

The crow paid no attention.

"Hey, Geena," she said in a loud, jaunty voice, "it's a *bird*. That's all. Only an old crow." She wanted to make herself laugh, but could not quite do it, and gave up the attempt.

A second crow arrived, settling down like an out-of-place shadow on the crabapple tree.

"Okay—two crows. They're still just birds," said Geena, beginning to falter as she went along. What was that movie her parents rented two months ago? Something done back in the sixties, she thought. A Hitchcock thriller, about birds. *The Birds*—that was the name of the movie. There were crows and seagulls on a jungle gym in a school yard that had made her want to scream.

A third crow arrived.

This wasn't funny anymore. Geena looked along one of the convergent paths and scowled. Was it her imagination, or was that particular walk darker than the other two? She turned around to the way she had come, and was satisfied that the path was well-lit. And the other path was almost as bright. But the third path was definitely darker.

A fourth and fifth crow came to join the first three.

Taking a chance, and fearful that if she didn't do something quickly she wouldn't be able to do anything at all, Geena all but flung a rust-colored ribbon at the edge of the darkest path and plunged down it. She made herself not look back, for fear she would see more crows gathering along the hedges. And she feared that the wind that had shaken the crabapple tree would pursue her.

Around her the darkness gathered, deepening, almost palpable in its density. It was more than shadow, and as Geena slowed her hectic pace, she began to wonder if this was some kind of manifestation of the ghost. After all she had been talking to it, trying to provoke it, maybe this was the result. This thought brought her up short, and she squinted ahead where the darkness seemed most dense, like a deep green syrup spread over the day. "Okay, ghost, if this is the way you want it," she declared, and pressed onward toward the gathering obscurity.

After a quick walk of ten minutes, she had made a number of turns in the path, and still was no closer to the eerie darkness than she had been when she first noticed it. This was not only scary, it was annoying. She wanted to stop and challenge the strange lack of light, but could not bring herself to do it. So she lengthened her stride and took the long breaths as she had been taught on the four-hour hikes at summer camp two years ago. "I can wait you out, ghost," she said, wishing she truly believed this was so.

Five minutes later she came to another junction, and this time made a point of fixing a rust-colored ribbon to the way she had come. The light was still oddly dark, like the day of a partial eclipse. There was a sulfurous tinge to the edge of the shadows and the light played tricks as it filtered through the dense leaves of the boxwood hedges that made up the maze. She shaded her eyes with her hand and squinted upward in the hope of finding the brilliant band of sunlight that had marked the progress of the day on the maze walls. But the sharp demarcation had faded, and a high, diffuse glare turned the shadows uncertain and the sky brassy. The quality of color around her was changing, going from bright olive greens and emeralds against the vivid sky to a deep shade of bottle-green contrasting to the high, metallic haze.

The junction was an irregular shape, not as ordered as the others had been. Geena wished she knew if this was a good sign or a bad one. She walked around the trapezoidal clearing, her shoulder brushing the walls of the maze as she went. At each of the paths, she paused and looked down them, wondering which way to go now. The odd daytime darkness around her troubled her more than she wanted to admit, and she made herself move cautiously. "Think," she ordered herself. "Think."

As she reached the path she had come on, she noticed that something strange was happening a short way back along it. The line of the hedges was not as sharp, and a certain fuzziness of appearance was changing the maze from a triumph of order to a neglected wilderness, where the paths were distorted by encroaching roots and branches, and the top of the maze was an uneven tangle.

"Oh, no, no. No you don't," said Geena. She realized that

102

some part of the maze was about to vanish into that non-place of gray mist, and she didn't want to be part of it. "Hey! Ghost! Ghost!" she shouted, wanting to make her protest before the mist came. If only she had something that could create some real noise now, like a high-power boombox, or a set of orchestral cymbals, or a gong. Those would surely demand the ghost's attention long enough to preserve the maze as it was when she entered it. If, indeed, it had not already changed beyond any possibility of return to Crispin and his Aunt Lucrece.

The hedges continued to encroach, and Geena grew giddy with fear. Much as she thought Crispin a snob and a wimp, she wouldn't have said no to his company right now. When they had left the tower yesterday, she had not felt so lost, so completely abandoned as she did now.

Maybe, she thought, maybe this happens to kids all the time. People think they run away or are kidnapped, or things you hear on the news. But maybe they were disappearing into paintings and videos and books. It was possible, if other kids could do what she could do. They would not be found because no one knew where to look. *And what then?*

Well, she decided, waiting here wasn't doing her any good. Better to be up and moving, doing something other than lingering here while the boxwood hedges closed in. She pulled another rust-colored ribbon from her sack and tied it to the entrance to the path that was still fairly clear, and started off down it, holding the handles of the sack firmly over her shoulder. She did her best not to run.

This path was not as easily negotiated as the others had been. Geena picked her way, so alert she was jumpy. The rustling of the leaves implied hidden danger. Small sounds seemed as ominous as gunfire. From time to time un-trimmed branches slapped at her, and once she nearly tripped over a stone on the path. The shadowy dapple of light overhead was still fading as the gray mist drew nearer.

A sharp caw caught her attention again. A crow was fly-ing directly above her, the black wings sawing at the air.

From this angle, Geena thought it looked huge, casting a shadow the size of a bus, as if a pterodactyl were overhead and not a crow.

"Go away!" she commanded, for all the good it did. This was more worrisome than Geena wanted to admit, for she could not rid herself of the certainty that the crow was watching her, responding to what she did, and perhaps causing her to do ill-considered things.

The crow continued on ahead, a mocking guide for Geena to follow—not that she had much choice. The path was so narrow now that she was having to use her arms to push leaves and branches out of her way. She would have cuts and bruises as well as sore muscles. This was not only a frightening place, she decided, it was making her very angry. Whatever the maze was doing, or whatever the ghost was up to, she had had her fill of it.

Finally she stumbled into another junction, this one fairly good-sized, with two cherry trees standing in it, one of them showing signs of leaf curl, the other apparently healthy. A small fountain in the shape of a leaping salmon spouted water from its mouth. There was a coating of green algae where the water dripped. She looked around, and was stuck by a thought. "How will I know when I reach the center of the maze?" she asked aloud, as if hoping for an answer. "Is there some kind of sign, or an announcement, or do I have to guess?"

The crow dropped down onto an unpruned branch in the boxwood hedge. It watched Geena closely, as if trying to decide if she was edible. It cawed twice in a muffled way, the sound reminding Geena of a rake on bricks, or a fingernail on a blackboard.

She noticed it carried something in its beak. At first she though it was a worm or perhaps a large insect, or a couple of twigs. Then, as she peered up at the crow, she realized the things in its beak were several rust-colored ribbons.

15

Outrage welled up in Geena faster than fright. How dare that bird remove her marker-ribbons! It was bad enough having the birds follow her, but this was too much. She found a large pebble and threw it at the crow, swearing the way the boys at school did when they played basketball and failed to score.

Another crow joined this first, this one with another ribbon held as a trophy—a light blue one.

A third and fourth crow were flying this way, with more to come.

"Just dandy," said Geena to the birds, using her grandmother's favorite expression of exasperation. It was better than sitting down and crying, which part of her wanted to do. "Do that later," she said to herself, wiping her eyes and staring up at the crows. "Cry when you're out of here, Geena." She knew it was good advice, but she wasn't sure she could wait so long.

Half a dozen more crows arrived, four of them with ribbons in their beaks. They settled on the branches of the overgrown boxwood and seemed prepared to stay as long as Geena did.

Never before had Geena understood why some people were afraid of birds, but she surely knew now. *Would it be any better,* she asked herself, *if they were blue-grey mockingbirds, or pretty cedar waxwings?* Would she rather have the birds look charming or exotic? Would that make any difference? *Probably not,* she decided. Not if they were taking her ribbons that marked the way out. Little golden finches would be sinister if they took her ribbons.

The grayness was still advancing, but more slowly, as if

perhaps it would stop short of this junction. Geena didn't know whether to feel relieved or trapped. She looked down the paths again, and impulsively she chose one and made her way down it, going as quietly as she could, wanting to add nothing to the disturbances around her. She felt too much like an intruder already and she didn't want to make it any worse by causing more disruption than she had.

Her skirt snagged on a protruding branch, and as she bent to free it, she gasped. The color of her clothes was no longer green, but a soft, pearl-grey in sculptured velvet, and the cut was trumpet-shaped, with fanning gores below her knee. In other circumstances she might have found it pretty. Now it was dismaying.

"No!" Geena protested as she ran her hands over the luxurious fabric. She did not dare to touch her hair, not wanting to discover it had changed again, in spite of all her efforts.

As she freed her skirts, she heard the caw of an approaching crow.

It made no sense to run—she realized that even as she raced along the narrow, treacherous path. Foolish as it was, she had to be active, and running made her feel she was not so helpless as she feared. She felt her sleeve tear and once she stumbled and scraped her palm as she did her best to remain on her feet. As soon as she had regained her balance, she made herself slow to a jog. The sack over her shoulder felt as heavy as if it held anvils. "It won't do any good to fall and break something. Not here."

How long she ran she didn't know or care. The path snaked around, doubled back on itself and ended abruptly in a clearing with a statue of a young woman carrying a large water ewer on her shoulder, which served as a fountain, dropping a small stream into the marble pan at her feet. The sound of it was musical and monotonous at the same time. There were four marble benches in this clearing, which appeared to be as neat and well-kept as the maze had been when Geena first started into it. Brilliant afternoon sunlight flooded the clearing.

107

Geena dropped wearily onto one of the benches, the stone cool where she touched it. "No more jokes, okay?" she asked the air. "I'm not up for any more jokes. Or any more crows," she added as an afterthought.

This time when the wind picked up, the hedges moved with it, leaning together and murmuring like the sea.

"I'll take that as a good sign," Geena declared. Now that she was out of that peculiar stretch of maze, she thought she might be able to figure out how long she had been trying to find her way. The sun was about halfway down the sky, making it about three. At home, she realized, she would be getting out of school about now, if it weren't summer. As it was, she and Marinelle Hunt would probably be standing in line for a matinee at the theater complex at the mall. "Um," she said. "I never thought I'd miss movies—even bad movies—this much." Or all the fun that went with movies. She still liked Clint Eastwood, even though he was getting old, and looked as if he had got his skin one size too small for his skull—Eastwood and Tommy Lee Jones were special, of the older stars. Anne Zivnuska thought that of the older guys Harrison Ford was more fun, and swooned over Tom Cruise. Kevin Costner was Marinelle's favorite. Spike said Denzel Washington was the best. Geena had seen Judd Nelson once in person, when he had been in town filming a movie. He had been buying a magazine: she had thought he looked tired.

Tears welled in her eyes and she swallowed hard against them. It was terrible to think of a world without movie stars. Besides, Clint Eastwood wouldn't really come riding out of the sunset to save her. Nobody would. *There's no one to rescue you*, she thought. *Just me*. The idea was more terrifying than she had thought possible.

"This is silly," she said sternly. "You've got more important things to think about than movies, or what actor is popular. They can't do anything about what's going on here, even if it were a movie. This isn't *The Wizard of Oz* or anything like it. That's make-believe. This is real."

108

As if to confirm her words, there came the cawing of crows overhead, and the first winged shadows sailed toward her.

"Hey, I thought we agreed, no more crows," Geena said, feeling totally worn our all of a sudden. She had had such hopes for her explorations, and what did she have to show for it? The places where she'd skinned her palms were throbbing. She could tell she had a blister forming on the side of her little toe, and this bothered her as much as her predicament did. The pain of it demanded her attention as nothing else could. It would be folly to take off her shoe to look, because then she wouldn't want to put the shoe back on, and it would be reckless to walk around this place bare-foot. It was a bad situation all around.

Much as she wanted to blame the ghost for her problems, however, she could not. She had gone into the painting be-cause she wanted to. She had come into the maze because she thought she could find some answers here. If she got a blister doing it, it was her own damn fault. But it hurt.

That was another thing she missed—the first-aid kit in her locker. She hadn't wanted to take it to school because the other kids would make fun of it, but her mother had insisted. Now Geena wished she had it with her. She could use the bandages and the ointments to take care of not only the blister, but the scrapes on her hands and the cuts on her arms. As it was, the best she could do was wash up, using water from the fountain. If Crispin were here, she thought, he would have something smart to say. So it was probably just as well she was alone. It was bad enough contending with crows. Putting up with Crispin would be too much.

These reflections didn't reassure Geena as much as she wanted them to. Truth to tell, she would have been glad of any company right now, even Eddie Howard, who had computers on the brain and thought all girls were crazy.

"Considering what's happening, maybe Eddie's right. This has all been pretty crazy. Like *Alice in Wonderland or Time Raiders*," Geena said, and made a botch of laughing at herself. This was not only not a movie, it wasn't a book or a video game, either. Reluctantly she got up and went to the statute, holding her hands out to the stream that splashed from the ewer. She missed Crispin almost as much as she missed her own family.

The cut on her upper arm where her sleeve had torn was still bleeding a bit, and her left palm was more abraded than the right, the skin at the base of her thumb looking like it had been gone over with scouring pads. Geena winced as she did her best to clean up, using the napkin from her sack for a towel. She didn't try to do anything about the blister.

"Time enough for that if it pops," she said as she went back to the bench and sat down again. "I'll take until the sun drops level with the hedge," she said decidedly. "And then I'll start out again."

She would have to retrace her steps, but once she was back in the unkept part of the maze, what then? The crows had taken her ribbons, so she would not be able to find her way back as she had planned to do if she had to. Without the ribbons she could wander about in the maze for hours and hours. There were so many little paths to get lost in. And her food wouldn't last much longer than breakfast tomorrow.

That thought of breakfast reminded her of the wine Crispin had put in with the water. Wine had alcohol and alcohol killed germs. She could put some of it on her cuts, and her hands, and that would stop any infection. Or at least slow it down.

This, too, would be easier if I had someone here with her, to help her, or to encourage her, she thought as she steeled herself against what she was about to do. It was not easy to open the wine bottle, for although the cork had been pulled out halfway, her hands hurt as she tried to extract it from the narrow green neck. It would be so easy to stop trying, she knew, but she didn't.

The wine stung as she patted it on her arm and her hands. The napkin was stained by it, and the smell of it

110

seemed unusually sharp. Or maybe that was the result of putting the wine on her broken skin.

Geena knew it would take a little time for the pain to subside, and so she lay back on the bench with the lumpy sack for a pillow, and let her mind drift. Without intending to, in a short while she was dozing, and after that she was asleep.

16

Crisp, hard footsteps awakened her suddenly almost an hour later, bringing her out of a shapeless and terrifying dream that made her think of women in bustles with parasols in their hands, all in summer white. What should be so unnerving about that fashion, Geena could not say, but the dread the dream inspired lingered as she tried to shake off her vestiges of sleep.

She turned her head without rising, and saw two neat, cloven hooves, and legs similar to a goat's all covered in curling russet hair. *But goats,* she thought, *have four legs, and this* . . . She raised her eyes and saw the hair give way to a naked torso, very human, with slender, strong arms, and a face that was familiar.

"Crispin!" she cried, shocked at the short beard and horns, just like the ones she had seen on the statue of the faun.

"Hello," said the faun, his voice nothing like Crispin's at all, but pleasantly raspy, and low enough to make it clear he was fully grown up. "Are you the one who's been running through the paths today?"

She didn't know how to answer that. "If you aren't Crispin, who are you?"

"I am . . . I suppose you may call me, oh, Phaon will do. It's Greek, like me." He smiled at her, and his smile was nothing like Crispin's; his mouth didn't just turn up at the corners, it angled away from the middle, like the kind of smile little kids draw, V-shaped. His ears, Geena saw, were as pointed as Mister Spock's.

"Phaon," she said, the name coming awkwardly to her.

"I know you are Geena," the faun went on, looking intently at her. She could see he had a little tail like a goat at the base of his spine.

Suspicious of him, and still thinking that Crispin might be playing some kind of joke on her—though what he had done to his feet and legs to make them look this way, or how he got the tail, she couldn't imagine—she asked, "How do you know that?"

"You've been talking to yourself. Either your name is Geena or you have an invisible companion by that name who annoys you," said Phaon, and ended with another triangular smile.

"My name is Geena, you're right about that," she conceded, and rubbed her face the way she often did when she woke up and wanted to get her mind going. She glanced down and saw she was still in pearl-colored sculptured velvet. At least there were no new changes in her clothes. Perhaps the ghost had been too busy with the faun—or Crispin—to change her any more. She blurted out the first question that came to her. "What are you doing here?"

"Oh, I live here." He sauntered a bit closer to her. "Why did you come into the maze?"

"To look for the center," she replied. "I don't suppose you know where that is?"

"What do you expect? Of course I do," said Phaon a bit boastfully. "I know where everything is in the maze. Most of the time." This last addition came with a quick expression of chagrin that was banished at once with a dazzling smile. "I can take you there, if you want to go."

"I do want to reach the center," Geena admitted, and hoped the appearance of this faun would mean her luck was changing. *Because*, she thought, *if he truly does know everything about the maze, he can guide me out of it as well as take me to the center.* It wouldn't matter that the crows had taken her ribbons.

Phaon preened. "I'll take you there." He put his hand on his chest. "It isn't very far now. You've done a better job than most with searching."

Geena got off the bench, her spirits rising. "Then let's go right now," she said.

"No," said Phaon in a tone of such sternness that she was shocked. "Not to the center. Not yet."

"Why not?" Geena asked.

He avoided looking at her. "The way there isn't . . . ready."

"How can it not be ready?" Geena demanded, and then recalled the gray mist that she had seen earlier. "You mean it's not there?"

"It's . . . somewhere else," the faun admitted heavily. "But it will return shortly, when the sun is lower." He jumped up on the bench where she had lain, his cloven hooves making a loud tattoo on the marble.

"How can you be so sure?" Geena asked him, almost satisfied now that she was not still asleep and dreaming.

"Because once the paths are completely in shadow, they all return." He jumped agilely down. "Unless the whole thing vanishes. It does from time to time. It did just recently, but now it's back it will remain for a while. It always has before."

"That's comforting," said Geena sarcastically to hide the discouragement that was taking hold of her again. "How long will we have to wait until the sun is low enough?"

"Oh, not so very long. And I can show you some of the tricks the maze has. You've already seen the part that looks overgrown," he added as if this would gain her consent to the adventure more quickly.

"That's deliberate?" asked Geena. "I thought mazes weren't supposed to be . . . like that."

"This one is," said Phaon with obvious pride.

"So I gather," said Geena. She reached out for her sack and was about to sling it over her shoulder again when she noticed that Phaon was shaking his head.

"You won't need that," he told her confidently.

"Maybe not, but I think I'll take it along. Habit." She stared at him. "You might not need food and water, but I do."

"But we won't be gone that long. I'll take you to the center, and then out again," he promised her with such sincerity that Geena found she could not believe him at all. "Truly."

That convinced Geena that he was up to something. She shook her head. "I want to have it with me. Just in case."

He made a face at her. "If you don't trust me . . ."

Although she didn't, she said, "It's not you, Phaon, it's this place. Since I got to this place yesterday, things keep changing on me. Can you blame me if I want to have something dependable with me?"

His smile was back full force. "What makes you think that the sack can't change? It could turn into almost anything, couldn't it?"

"I guess," she said, not wanting to admit it. "But so far it hasn't, and it's about the only thing that hasn't."

"You're being foolish." Phaon was beginning to disapprove of her.

"Indulge me," said Geena with temper sharpening her request.

Quite suddenly he shrugged. "If you want to burden yourself unnecessarily, that's your concern. Take anything you want. Carry one of the benches if it suits you." He scampered a short distance away and bounded back toward Geena. "But you'll have to move quickly if you're going to catch up with me."

"I thought you wanted my company," Geena countered, determined not to put herself too much in the faun's hands. "If you don't, I'll do what I can on my own. You said yourself I had done fairly well."

For a moment he was flustered. "But it'll be sunset in two or three hours. And then what will you do? You didn't plan to sleep in the maze, did you?"

"I didn't plan to spend any time here at all," said Geena hotly. "I thought I could just look around and leave." Saying this much aloud brought on a wave of apprehension that brought her perilously close to tears. She fought to hold them off. "Besides, I have a blister on my foot, so I can't go real fast."

"With such shoes, I'm not surprised," said Phaon unsympathetically as he regarded her walking shoes. "But if you really have a blister, I won't make you run." He smirked. "Hooves are better in this place."

"I bet they are," she said. "But I have feet and shoes, and that's that." She folded her arms, one hand through the handles of the sack to hold it in place.

He relented. "Very well, then. Follow me, and don't let me get too far ahead." He leaped away back the way she had come. "The dead ends are almost more interesting than the center. Come on." He scampered down the path a short way ahead of her.

"Don't get too far ahead," she reminded him as she went after him, doing her best not to limp, recalling what her track coach, Miz Lake had said last year during the track meet: *It's going to hurt whether you limp or not, and limping makes for more sore muscles—so don't limp if you can help it.* She had made it work then. She would make it work now.

Phaon ambled back toward her, mischief in his golden eyes. "I could carry you if you put the sack down."

"Thanks. I'll manage," she said brusquely. "And you're the one who warned me to keep you nearby."

"So I did," he said, bowing to her with a courtliness that would have surprised her if she had not prepared herself for all sorts of shenanigans from Phaon. From their short acquaintance she had realized he was prankish and very likely unreliable. In fact, she wasn't certain it was good sense to follow him at all, but with her ribbons gone and the day getting late, she had no better ideas.

"You'll see. This is not such a bad place." He rushed ahead and came back in her direction. "At the junction up ahead, go to the right. I think you'll be surprised at what you find." With that, he leaped into the air and was far ahead of her before she could speak.

It was all she could do not to cry out in protest, but,

guessing that was what he sought, Geena kept her mouth closed, and upbraided herself inside for letting the faun trick her as he had.

"But," she said to herself as she continued to walk, every other step lancing a sharp pain from the outside of her little toe that traveled up her leg to her jaw. "I would have had to turn around and come back this way anyway, so it isn't Phaon's fault. He's playing games, that's all."

She reached the junction, and for a short while stood wondering if she should do as Phaon had told her, or go on the other path. But the gray mist had been there, she recalled, and that worried her more than the rambunctious faun did. With the sun dropping lower in the sky, the maze had come alive with shadows.

"Why didn't Crispin give me a candle and some matches? He tried to think of everything else. Why not those? And bandages?" she asked the glowing sky overhead that was already changing from blue to pale gold toward the west. She answered the question for herself, knowing it was the only sensible explanation: "Because neither of you thought you'd need it."

"Why not?" Phaon's question came so quickly and so near at hand that Geena all but jumped sideways.

"Where have you been?" she demanded, and hated herself for asking him.

"Watching you," he answered. "It's easy when you know the maze well." He chuckled at her consternation. "I watch people all the time. Mostly gardeners, of course. But there are others as well."

"And where are they now, these others?" Geena inquired in what she hoped was a sweet voice. "Or do you know?" Crispin had said there were people who had gone into the maze and had never been seen again. She didn't intend to be one of these if she could help it.

"They left. Everyone leaves," he said, and his face looked sad.

Afraid that the faun was using sympathy to gain the

upper hand again, Geena didn't let herself be drawn into the snare of feeling sorry for him. "If you feel that way, why do you remain?"

"Where could I go? To a carnival? To a rich patron with a houseful of dwarves and two-headed calves?" he shot back, the charm gone out of him as if he had been touched by a malign force. "It is better here in the maze, where I am able to live as I please. Or don't you want to be where you belong?" This last clever challenge caught her unprepared.

"Of course I want to go back," she shouted at him.

"Then you'd better come with me or you'll be wandering about here until midnight." His easy manner was back as if it had never left. He winked at her and bowed her toward the path he had told her to take.

Head high, Geena went in that direction, hoping she was doing the right thing. If Phaon wanted to make certain she was totally lost, this was his opportunity, she thought.

They went along for some distance, Phaon still in the lead, but keeping to the pace that Geena set. He glanced up from time to time, but whether he was watching the sky or for crows, she could not say.

At last they came to another dead end, this one star-shaped with a wisteria tree growing in its center. Only a few, faded blossoms remained, but the tree was still quite pretty, a lovely shape, the spreading, drooping branches held up by an elaborate trellis.

"This is very nice," said Geena, wishing she had found this earlier in the day so that she could have seen it in better light.

"It's fairly new. There used to be a willow here, but it was cut down some time ago." He posed under the wisteria.

"You mean it didn't just change from a willow to a wisteria?" Geena asked, surprised that anything so mundane could happen here. "Parts of the castle come and go like bad rock bands, but a tree has to be cut down and a new one planted." She shook her head. "It sounds like too much work to me."

He glared at her. "The gardeners did this," he insisted.

"Okay, okay." She didn't want him to get mad at her. "I believe you."

"And they keep the avenues pruned. Or unpruned." He chuckled once. "You'd be surprised the number of people who think that the maze has been accidentally neglected in the overgrown parts." He flung out his arms. "If the maze were truly left to go wild, the paths would close up almost at once. The gardeners have instructions to make the maze a wilderness in places. Wild, but not so wild that you can't get through or find your way." He took real satisfaction in this.

"Why would they do this?" Geena asked.

"For fashion," said Phaon with a shrug that was so like Crispin that Geena wondered again if there was some connection between the two. Perhaps the ghost had done something to make a wild version of Crispin. Or a tame version of Phaon.

"What sort of fashion?" asked Geena, finding it hard to believe anyone would do this deliberately.

"The current one, of course. The one for ruins and castles, and romantic wildernesses. The British do the most with the fashion, but in this part of the world, those who can afford it have a place like this, where they can let nature run carefully riot." He came up to her side. "The fashion includes me."

"Oh?" said Geena, her worry about Phaon returning. "How is that?"

He touched her face and turned her head so she would have to look at him. His buzzy voice grew deeper and his golden eyes fixed on hers. "Fauns are very romantic. Didn't you know?" He bent and swiftly, lightly, kissed her at the corner of her mouth, moving so quickly that she could do nothing before it was done and felt silly doing something after. As he jumped back from her, he said, "Girls like you sometimes scream when I do that."

"Do you do it often?" she asked, trying to keep her bearing with him. She had seen boys like him, who knew they were cute and made the most of it with girls. The worst was Eric Clark, who had gorgeous blue eyes, red-brown hair, and played first trumpet in band. Marinelle had a crush on him, along with half the girls at Washington High. Phaon acted the same way.

"Not often enough," he answered, then edged away, as if he were more concerned with her reaction than she was. "Come with me, Geena. I'll show you another wonderful dead end."

"Why a dead end?" she asked, suspicious of his motives.

"Because you don't have anything better to do with your time, do you?" he inquired with what seemed like real kindness.

She shrugged, adjusting the sack handles at the same time. "Why not?" she said, preparing to follow him. "Unless we can get to the center of the maze now."

"Not yet. Soon," he said, and with a teasing smile led the way into another part of the maze.

17

Phaon led her to a charming artificial waterfall that was really a fountain. It was at the end of a dead end near the outside wall of the maze, Phaon talking all the while about the trouble the ghost caused in the maze. "This is one of the places that doesn't often change," he said as he stood aside so she could admire the place.

"It's very pretty," said Geena. She meant every word of it.

The fountain had been laid out and planted to create the impression of a spring in a forest glade, with ferns trailing their delicate fronds in the water like green tresses. A number of flowering shrubs and a patch of spiky, fragrant rosemary completed the setting.

"This is one of the best fountains, I think, though not the most spectacular. The moat feeds the waterfall," he said as he indicated the structure.

"The *moat*?" Geena all but yelled at him. "The moat is nearby?"

"Sometimes," he answered obliquely, not looking directly at her. "In the morning, but the maze . . ." He seemed confused now. He began to wander away from her as if seeking the means to escape.

Geena pursued him. "Tell me about the moat," she demanded, getting as close to him as she felt was safe to do. "I have to know about it, Phaon. Really I do. It's important."

"It's just a moat, with water lilies—" he began only to be cut off.

"I *know* that. I got here by crossing it. But I have to find out about where it is, when it's around," she said impatiently. "Anything you can tell me that will help me find it when I can cross it again . . ." She faltered.

His gave her his attention with more seriousness. "Well, it's large. And most days until early afternoon it lies next to the castle. It vanishes in the middle of the afternoon if it's going to vanish at all." He paused, and then added, as if to give her a treat, "Most of the time it's covered in water lilies."

"I know that, too," said Geena, her temper showing. "And I have to get back across it."

He shook his head. "Not tonight. Tonight the moat isn't there."

"How do you know?" she persisted. "Do you keep track of it?"

"Of course I do," he said as if offended. "What else would I do with my time if not that?"

Geena shrugged. "Is that what fauns do?" she asked. "Patrol mazes?"

"It is what *I* do." He gave her a defiant look, and again his charm vanished to be replaced by a display of sharp temper. "I do not sit under trees all day eating fruit and playing my pipes to entertain the shepherdesses. No matter what you may have heard about such things."

"I've always wondered what *taking umbrage* meant," said Geena with a geniality that was as false as it was polished. "Now I know. It's when you get all offended and huffy."

"That isn't the case," said Phaon. "You were insulting me."

"I was not," said Geena stubbornly. The pain had spread from her blister so now it felt that her foot was one continuous ache; it made her testy. "I don't know why I should bother talking to you about any of this. You aren't going to help me anyway, are you?" She was secretly pleased to see him flinch.

"Why should I, when you show me so much contempt?" he shot back, anger turning his gracefulness to menace.

Geena remembered being told in her Anthropology for Kids Summer Seminar that the Greek woodland figures, like fauns, were mythological cousins to werewolves, and represented the wildness in human nature. They were supposed

122

to remind people of the animal within themselves. She had thought she knew what that meant, but until this moment, she had not truly grasped its full implication. Now she had to fight the urge to run, fearing that flight would do nothing more than spur him to violence. "It isn't contempt," she said as if she were talking to one of those boys in a street gang, "it's that I've never known anyone like you before."

This apparently was the response he was seeking. His mercurial smile returned at once. "Actually, I'm unique," he said proudly. "Not many people have ever seen anything like me, not in this part of the world." He spread his hand on his chest, as if posing for a picture.

"That you are," said Geena at once, glad to have stumbled upon a way to keep order with the two of them. *Flattery seems to work quite well,* she thought. Her mother had told her a year ago that all boys like compliments no matter how much they tell you they don't. "You're much better looking than the statue of you."

Now he beamed. "I think so, too. The statue lacks animation."

Geena covered a spurt of laughter in time as she realized that Phaon meant animation in the sense of vitality, not cartoons. "Yes, it does," she agreed.

He took her amusement as a favorable sign. "Animation is always a thing to be desired," he said, making the words as suggestive as possible. He leaned his head back so that the short curls of his beard angled at the fading sky. "It will be a beautiful night."

"If the mist stays away," Geena said with more feeling than she expected to have. "In a place like this one, you can't be sure about the night, can you?"

"You might not be able to be sure, but I can," said Phaon, his tongue flicking out between his teeth. He looked at her from the tail of his eye. "How much do you know about the mist?"

"Enough to know I don't like it," she said with unexpected firmness. "It takes you away from here and leaves you where there is nothing." As she spoke she glanced around uneasily. "This place is . . ."

"Strange," he finished for her when she didn't go on. "I have heard many of those coming into the maze say that. Some of them ended up cursing the place after two or three hours here." He sidled toward her. "What will you do if the mist comes?"

"Get mad, probably," she said.

"I could help you," Phaon offered.

"How?" she asked bluntly.

"Oh, I could keep you with me. I always stay with the maze, mist or clear. I don't change like the rest." He was boasting again, but Geena was fairly certain he was also telling her the truth.

But Geena wanted no part of it. "What would you do with me around? Tell me that. Wouldn't I change, whether you did nor not?" she asked him. "Wouldn't I be a risk to you?" She had no intention of ending up a garden decoration in this maze with the moat near enough to smell.

"I don't . . ." he began, then stared off into the gathering darkness. "You might be a hazard."

"Has anyone ever stayed with you before now?" Geena asked, trying to sound more apprehensive for him than for herself.

"No. Not through the mist and the other place," he admitted reluctantly. "And no one has ever remained—"

"Unchanged?" she suggested. "Doesn't that worry you? Aren't you afraid of what they could mean to you, all these changes?" She took advantage of the doubt she saw in his eyes. "You say you haven't changed. I say you haven't changed *yet*. And if you take the chance of protecting me, you might be exposing yourself to more trouble than you can imagine. The ghost moves this maze around often, I've been told, and not just by you. They told me that in the castle."

"Yes," he said guardedly, not following Geena's thoughts. "It does."

"And you say you remain with the maze," she said, wishing she had a sense of how he might react to what she planned to say. "And if the ghost moved the maze to a place where you would not belong, what would happen to you then? And would it be fair of me to make you go to such a place?"

There was no jauntiness in him now, and not a trace of good humor. "That wouldn't happen."

"Are you certain?" she asked, for as much as she longed for company, she dreaded what could become of her in this maze, especially once the mist reached the heart of it and moved it to the other place where there was only gray mist.

"Naturally," he said, head up again, and his attitude one of innate superiority.

"Well, I'm not," she said to him, and flung one hand up at the sky. "Once the light's gone, who knows what will happen to you or to me? I don't think it makes a lot of sense to—"

"I can protect you," he insisted, his jaw set in an uncompromising line that the curl of his beard emphasized. "If you stay with me, you'll be safe. If you don't, who knows what will become of you?"

"Who knows?" she agreed, her courage almost failing her again. "But that doesn't mean I'm going to be lost without you."

Four crows arrived at the edge of the clearing, one of them settling onto a tree near the waterfall-fountain, the rest finding perches in the hedges.

Phaon glowered at the crows, and made a half-hearted rush toward the one near the fountain. His mouth had turned sullen now.

"See what I mean?" said Geena. "You're not in charge here. Neither am I."

"The ghost doesn't own the crows," Phaon insisted. "They fly around as they wish." He studied her a short while. "Why do you think you can manage to take care of yourself?"

"Because I have to. No one else can," said Geena, hating

125

the way that sounded, for it made her feel more vulnerable than she had ever felt in her life. She was aware he would not like this response and so she did what she could to soften its blow. "Thank you for offering to help me. If I thought it would work, I would accept your offer at once, but—"

"You don't think I can do it, do you?" he demanded, lengthening his stride as he made his way around the limits of the dead end clearing.

"I don't know if you can or you can't. And that isn't good enough." This last made her feel very much alone.

Suddenly his expression went crafty. "I know where the moat is. I can find it for you."

"If the maze is in the right place to do it," she reminded him. "And you can't be sure it will be, can you? You can stay with me, but you can't guarantee where we'll be." The sinking feeling was back behind her ribs again. This was turning out to be harder than she thought it would be.

He laughed at her and the sound was feral, the kind of laugh a wolf might make, or a raccoon. "You will be on your own." He was standing deep in the shadow of the boxwood hedge, a pale smear in the gathering darkness.

"I guess I will," she said, disliking the idea intently.

The laughter came again, and then faded quickly. Where Phaon had been standing there were now only rustling shadows.

Geena peered into the dusk but could not see the faun against the greater umbra of the hedges. She took a few, tentative steps toward where he had been, then stopped and called his name, softly at first, and then more loudly as she circled the clearing. "Hey, Phaon, this is getting scary. Come out!"

The only response she received was a sound that might have been his fading laughter.

She stood by herself with the night encroaching around her. As it sunk in on her that Phaon had actually left her, she had to think hard to keep from crying. This time it didn't work as well as she hoped. She sat down on one of the small boulders beside the fountain and wept, her hands held to her face in spite of the sting her tears gave to her injured palms.

Some time later, when she had stopped crying, she pulled her sack off her shoulder and opened it, feeling around inside for the remaining food. By the time she had assembled the makings of a small supper, the moon, not quite full, had swung into the sky and was beginning its journey across the night.

"All in all," said Geena to give herself some comfort, "not too shabby for a nighttime picnic."

18

Her dreams were fitful, with images of her mother calling for her, and her father talking to cops. Geena watched her dream-self struggle to reach her family without success, caught up in a vortex that carried her to more distant places than the countryside of France a century ago. The worst part of it was that not only was the dream-Geena lost, she was turning into someone who wasn't Geena, and this was far more frightening than anything she had to face in the dream, no matter how eerie it was. Intermixed with these images were vistas of castles rising out of the mists only to be dissolved, hedges that moved and grabbed, gigantic crows pursuing running people, a boy who was both Crispin and Phaon, the presence of a whimsical ghost, and the constant unpleasant sensation of cold and hardness brought about by sleeping on the ground.

Geena wakened at the base of a peach tree in a vast orchard, the sound of bees droning above her. The first thought that crossed her waking mind was: *at least they're not crows.* The morning was brilliant, the sky so blue it looked as if someone had spent the night polishing it. As she rubbed her eyes, she could tell she was still Geena, and that was the best discovery in all her time in the painting.

Wishing she had a comb and a toothbrush, Geena did what she could to set herself in order. She raked her fingers through her hair and was relieved to discover it hadn't grown or fallen out during the night. She couldn't tell from touching it what color it might be. Her clothes were still pearl-colored sculptured velvet. "Either the ghost hasn't got around to me yet, or he doesn't care right now how I look."

She got up and looked around but could not find the

castle. Either it had disappeared or she was too far away from it to see it. Or maybe it was on the other side of all the orchard trees, and they screened the castle from view.

The last of the bread was hard, but she ate it, along with the single remaining apple. She balked at eating mustard without anything to put it on other than bread. Though she was out of food, there were peaches ripe enough to eat on the trees. She wouldn't go hungry, not for fruit. With a sigh she looped the handles of the sack over the limb of the nearest peach tree. The bottles and jars were carefully stored in it. "Maybe someone from the castle will find it," she said, thinking it would be nice if they found her as well. She looked around for the fountain of the night before, but could not find it, though she heard the distant gurgle of water. Having no better idea in mind, she began to walk through the orchard toward the sound. If nothing else, she was thirsty.

As she walked, many things flitted through her mind. There was a soccer match next Saturday and she was supposed to play in it. Uncle Pete was supposed to have a barbecue at his house on Sunday: if she was still gone, they'd probably cancel it. At home this afternoon Stephanie Henderson's mother was supposed to give a talk to the neighborhood committee on proper exterior lighting for house safety. Stephanie's mom was a cop. Until a couple days ago, Geena had thought that sounded exciting, catching crooks and helping people. Now she thought it must be a pretty ordinary job most of the time. Not that it wasn't dangerous, but it didn't have to do with ghosts or any of the other strange things she had encountered in the last two days. A cop, like a movie star, wouldn't help much here.

She had sore muscles from sleeping on the ground, her scraped palms were tender, and her blister still hurt, but she realized that although she didn't like any of it much, she could deal with it if she had to.

The orchard was large and sprawling. Walking through it, Geena had the strong sensation it was about the same size as the maze. "Maybe," she said aloud, "it is where the maze was. When the garden goes, and the topiary isn't around, maybe the orchard is." It made as much sense as anything else did in this place. She decided to test her theory, and tried to estimate the locations in the maze in relation to the orchard. Now that she was out of the thing, she was annoyed that she had never found its center.

"Maybe it didn't have one," she said aloud. "This is the kind of place that would have a maze without a center." She heard birdcalls and looked up, half-expecting to see crows. But there were only small, taupe-colored birds with a lovely, liquid song. "You keep at it," she told the birds. She hoped there would be no crows to ruin the morning.

The gurgle of water was nearer, but she could not see any of it. "This better not be another joke, ghost," she warned, realizing as she went on that the day was getting quite warm. The canopy of leaves protected her from the full weight of the strengthening sun, but it also kept the air close, like an invisible blanket. By afternoon it would be muggy. The smell, too, was earthy and green, with the sweet scent of ripening peaches over all the rest.

Then she heard a sound not far from her, not the chuckle of water, but the definite sound of a grown man clearing his throat.

Surely it wasn't Crispin or Phaon. This noise was too much like the way her dad sounded in the morning before he started shaving. Maybe it was the gardener, she thought. Maybe it was someone who had been watching her—that notion was upsetting.

Maybe it was the ghost.

There came another confused collection of noises. Geena stopped walking and cocked her head to listen. Then, very carefully, she made her way toward the sound, doing her best to move from the shelter of one peach tree trunk to another.

At the edge of the orchard, facing the bend of a stream, Geena saw a blocky, middle-aged man with a short, well-

trimmed dark beard, and dark hair covered by a wide-brimmed straw hat. A linen jacket was hanging on the limb of a tree, and he was just pulling a paint-stained cotton smock over his head, and having some difficulty with the hat.

In spite of her intentions to keep silent, Geena laughed. Then she clapped her hands over her mouth as if to deny what she had done.

The man was startled, he turned quickly and his hat fell off, showing a receding hairline. He looked about sharply, his eyes taking in everything as he stared at the orchard. "Who's there?" he rapped out as he bent to recover his hat. Beside him was a kind of stand with an odd suitcase atop it, standing open.

Geena said nothing. She looked over her shoulder and wondered if she could get away without being seen.

"I know you are there," the man went on. "What are you doing in my orchard? Stealing peaches?"

"No," she answered indignantly. After all she had gone through here, to be called a peach thief by a man in a straw hat was too silly or too humiliating to tolerate.

"Then show yourself," he ordered, folding his arms.

Deciding he wasn't too dangerous, Geena stepped forward. "It's just me."

He stared at her. "But who . . ." Then recognition came into his eyes. He made an abrupt gesture of vexation. *"You.* You're the one who's been insinuating yourself into all my sketches and studies. What do you have to say for yourself?"

"Insinuate?" she repeated, alarmed at his accusation. "I did not."

He was unimpressed. "I can show you," he said, and reached for an old-fashioned portfolio leaning against the trunk of the tree where his jacket hung. "It's in my sketches. You'll see." He untied the closures and drew out a bound, oversized book, staring down at the pages as he flipped through them. "There! You see?" He held the book out to her. "Look for yourself. This is yesterday. And this the day before."

132

Geena permitted her curiosity to get the better of her. She stepped forward and took the sketchbook in her hands. "What do you mean?" she asked, trying not to upset him any more than she already had.

"Look," he commanded, pointing down at the open page. "There. And there. Any idiot can—"

But Geena was staring at the sketch, not aware of the figure in the scenery, of a formal garden, astonished by the heading on the page. *Giverny*, it read. *August, 1893.* She could not take her eyes off the name of the village, nor the date. She looked up at the man, undaunted by his forbidding expression. "You're Claude Monet, aren't you?" The only photograph she had seen of him was taken when he was an old man, with a large white beard, a bald pate, moustache still dark, looking like Santa Claus in a three-piece suit. But he hadn't always been that way, she realized as she goggled at him. Once, in the 1890s, he had been middle-aged. "I can't believe this. You're my very favorite artist." It came out in a gush and she felt her cheeks redden at her own enthusiasm.

The man unbent a little. "I am Monet, yes." And then, as if good manners demanded it, he asked, "And who are you?"

"Geena," she said, her voice squeaking. "Geena Howe. I can't tell you . . ." This was the most unreal event amid all the unbelievable events that had occurred since she crossed the moat into this world. "It's . . . just great to meet you. I can't tell you . . . I've liked your stuff since I was a little kid . . ." She knew she was babbling but couldn't stop. "I guess I shouldn't call it 'stuff', huh? I love your work. I really do. . . . That's better, isn't it?" Her hands were shaking so badly that she nearly dropped the sketchbook. "This is for real, isn't it . . . ? I mean, this isn't some kind of art theme park, is it? And you're not a hologram or some kind of audio-animatronic. You're really here. This isn't virtual reality, is it?"

He regarded her with a bemused stare. "What are you talking about, young lady?"

"Oh, oh, God, I'm not making any sense, am I?" She

clung to the sketchbook as if it could protect her. What did he know about special effects, computers, holograms, and the rest of it? According to his sketchbook it was August in 1893, in a French country village not far from the Seine. It was real. She hadn't been making it up. Now that she knew this, she realized that she had been comforting herself with the possibility that it was actually a dream, or something in her imagination. But the sketchbook changed all that. "You'd better take it before I drop it."

He reached out and reclaimed it, then returned it to the portfolio. "Will you believe it?—I do not precisely understand yet. What are you doing in my orchard?"

She made a gesture of helplessness. "I don't know. It was a maze yesterday. And the day before it was a topiary garden. A lot smaller than this." As she said it she knew it made no sense. With an effort she tried to explain. "I was looking at one of your *Water Lilies* studies, two days ago. I like to look at it—"

He interrupted her. "Why should you be looking at my sketches? And how," he went on in a more accusatory way, "did you come to have your hands on them?"

"Not a sketch," she said impatiently, afraid that he was kidding her for an artisty reason all his own. "A painting. A large painting. It's one of several." She couldn't believe he had forgotten such impressive works. "A huge pond of water lilies."

"About so by so?" he asked, holding up his hands and indicating an imaginary frame of about eighteen by twenty inches. "Of the pond across from my house?"

"No," she said, unnerved by his question. "No. Nothing like that. Very big. Maybe eight or nine feet long and six feet high. Something like that. Not any smaller, I'm sure of it." She waited for his response, then prompted him. "They're famous all over the world."

A slight smile appeared at the corners of his mouth. "Are they?"

"Yes," she said with great sincerity. "They're *beautiful*."

"That's very encouraging to know," he said, a hidden amusement making his eyes brighter than before. He indicated what at first glance appeared to be a bundle of sticks on the ground. "But charming as this discussion is, if you are so fond of my paintings you must excuse me. I have work to do." Saying this, he retrieved the bundle of sticks and began to set up his easel.

Geena didn't want to go, but she realized she ought to. But how to get back to the castle? "Pardon me, Mr. Monet—I can't believe it's really you—but can you tell me how I can get back to the castle with a tower? I was there yesterday—"

"I know you were," he said, perturbed. The easel was in place and now he was reaching for a mounted canvas in his portfolio. "And I hope you will not interfere with me today."

"Oh." She hesitated. "The thing is, I don't know this area. The castle—can you tell me where to find it?" she asked, as deferentially as possible.

"What are you talking about?" he asked her. "Is this supposed to be amusing?"

Geena could see no reason for his being affronted, and would have said so if she hadn't wanted the information so much. "Not to me. I don't know where the castle is. And I have some things there I want to get. I left them when I arrived." What would happen if she couldn't find the castle again? Would that mean she wouldn't be able to cross the moat? Or, since the moat wasn't in the painting itself, would she be able to leave without finding the castle again?

He set the canvas on the easel. "The tower is on the Seine. The castle is about a half hour's walk the other side of Giverny." He pointed to the canvas and the partially finished painting. "And it's here, of course."

This caught Geena's attention at once, and the last part of the puzzle clicked into place. She took an inadvertent step forward as the whole of her plight rushed in on her. Turning from the painting to Monet, she announced, *"You're the ghost!"*

19

"Ghost?" he repeated incredulously. "No such thing. There is no ghost. What are you talking about now? More tales of paintings I do not know." He continued to prepare to paint, selecting his brushes and colors with care. He was almost ignoring her. "I must work now. I will lose the light if I don't."

"That castle is haunted," Geena said forcefully. "I know. I've been in it and I've seen the haunting. Whole parts of the place vanish in light gray mist and then become something else. And the people change, too. Hair changes color, and clothes are different."

"Really," he said drily.

"Yes," she insisted. "You're haunting it."

"That's ridiculous," he said. In French it sounded much more condemning than in English. "Why should I haunt something I am painting?"

"I don't know, and it's not ridiculous. I've been in it. I should know." She looked at the canvas, at the portion that had been painted out. "Let me tell you what you had there, in that gray patch, day before yesterday. You had a cloister and a gallery connecting the castle to the tower, as if they were part of the same building. Then, when you'd finished work for the day, you changed your mind and painted it out. You had only a bit of the gallery left, like walls broken." She was speaking quickly, trying to recall everything she had seen in that odd mist. "I guess you scumbled white over what you had painted, and because of the colors beneath it looked gray. And you decided to make the distance between the castle and the tower wider, didn't you?"

"Yes. You're right." He was staring at her with obvious astonishment. "How do you know?"

"Because I was *in* it. That's how." She hoped he would not decide she was completely out of her mind. "And those drawings you showed me of the maze, the ones you said I was in, well, you're right. I spent all of yesterday afternoon in the maze. When I fell asleep, I was still there, in a dead end. I woke up in this orchard. And I do not sleepwalk, Mr. Monet. I got out of the maze because it disappeared, not because I found my way out." Again she was talking too fast, but if he would not be convinced by her arguments, he might be convinced by her speed. Surely she was going too quickly to be making it up. "Does it really have a center, or is it only a bunch of sketches and not an overall plan?"

He nodded. "You're right. I have not made a plan. I have been preparing some sketches of gardens at the castle you spoke of. I go there once or twice a week to sketch. The light changes so radically during the course of a day, particularly on the pruned hedges." He sounded distracted but his next inquiry was sharp. "There are statues on the grounds there. Tell me what they look like."

Knowing this was a crucial test, Geena said, "There is a leaping salmon with a fountain coming out of its mouth. There is a woman carrying some kind of water jug over her shoulder. There is a faun who looks like Crispin—"

"Who?" Monet asked.

"Crispin. You must know him," she answered. "I don't think he's one of your kids. He's too spooked about the castle. He lives there. About my age, reddish or blond hair most of the time, looks good in green and blue, kind of cute. Both Crispin and the faun. Called Phaon."

"Oh. You mean Albert," he said, pronouncing the name Ahl-BEHR. "The nephew of the—"

"Woman who owns the castle," Geena finished for him. "Lucrece, he called her. Is that her name?"

He shook his head. "She is Madame Violette Marais, a widow whose husband was a great man of business. He bought the old castle for her, to indulge her love of ancient things. And then he succumbed to pneumonia," said Monet with a short sigh, then added, "Yes, a most hospitable woman in spite of her misfortunes. Just at present she is taken by the fashion for things medieval; she's as bad as those English Morris has around him. No matter. She has given me run of her gardens." He smiled at Geena. "You are a very intriguing young woman, Mademoiselle Howe."

"Does her house have the moat?" Geena interjected, as much because flattery from Claude Monet embarrassed her as because she wanted her adventure to end.

"Not much of one, but yes, it has a moat," he said to her indulgently.

"With water lilies?" Geena pursued.

"Yes, with water lilies," he confirmed, and continued with growing cordiality, "It was her house, incidentally, that inspired me to make my own pond across the road from my house." At last he gave her a sign of approval. "All right. I do not know how you managed it, but it appears that somehow you have, indeed, ended up in my paintings and sketches. So if anyone is haunting this place, it is you, young woman. You are the interloper, not I." He stroked his beard. "I hardly know how to advise you. I have never encountered such a problem before."

Thinking of her early attempts with the Mondrian and the Vermeer, Geena said, "I don't actually know how I do it, but I've done it before. Not like this, though. They were just short experiments. This is more of an exploration. I think I'm improving."

"Do you?" He scrutinized her now, the speculative shine in his eyes at once a hopeful and a disquieting sign. "How do you manage it?"

She shrugged. "I don't quite know. It's a talent I have, is all. I look at the picture in a certain way for long enough, and then . . . I'm in it. I go into the painting. I did that here." Her smile was uncertain. "I didn't mean to cause any trouble. But the painting is so beautiful, and—"

"A very large painting of water lilies," he mused, a dreaminess in his eyes that made him seem far away.

"That's right. It's part of a series of water lily paintings." She looked directly at him. "Are you sure you don't remember?"

"I regret, Mademoiselle, I do not," he said as if he meant it.

"Well, I don't see how you could do that, but okay," she said, deciding that he didn't want to discuss the paintings with her. Some artists were like that, she knew from her reading. And some wanted to talk about nothing but their paintings. She would have to wait until he changed his mind and that, she feared, would be some time. Another, less welcome thought intruded—if he could not or would not remember the painting, didn't that mean she was stuck here? Much as she admired Monet's work, she felt upset by him.

"Is this a problem?" he asked, seeing how her expression clouded over. "That I do not recall the work you describe?"

"It may be," she said, and indicated the painting he had put on the easel. "Are you planning to put the moat in that?"

"I had not thought about it," he answered with scant attention. "I may. I may not."

"Okay. But if you do—"

"Why should I? What would be the significance to you if I paint this moat again or not? And why should the day matter to you?" He watched her, waiting for her answer.

She sighed. The time she had been gone from her home, which she had hoped was coming to an end now stretched ahead of her as vast as all the water lilies Monet painted over the years. What could she do to persuade him to help her? She decided she might try the truth. It couldn't hurt. Unless he decided she was one of those crazed fans who cause so much trouble. They might put her in a lunatic asylum. That thought made her wince. "Mr. Monet," she began, "I would like to get home. But I can't do it if I don't have the picture that brought me here."

"You mean a large painting of water lilies?" he asked and

shook his head. "No, Mademoiselle, I don't know what to tell you, for I fear I must disappoint you. I have no such canvases."

"I think all I need is the moat," she said. "The moat is real here, but if it is the right part of the moat, and the light strikes it right, I think I could go back." She was glad she didn't whine. She hated other girls' whining, and refused to do it herself.

He regarded her with a mixture of impatience and intrigue. "Clearly you have something in mind. What is it?"

"I . . . I don't know for sure, but . . ." Geena did not know how to continue, since her idea was only half-formed in any case.

"You might as well tell me," Monet said. "You won't leave me in peace until you do, will you?"

Geena felt shocked by this rebuke. "I . . . I don't mean to . . ."

He looked squarely at her. "But you have an idea. That much is obvious. You might as well tell me what it is."

She gathered up as much of nerve as she could and said, "It'll probably seem a little odd—"

"My dear young woman," said Monet in exasperation, "everything you've said so far has been more than a little odd. I quail at the thought of discovering what seems odd to you." He folded his arms and waited.

He really is imposing, thought Geena as she looked from Monet to his canvas. "Yesterday, when you were working on the maze, it was here."

"Yes," he said, with a note of doubt in his voice. "You have persuaded me that you know the maze."

She put her hand to her forehead. "You have to believe me that I was in the middle of what you were painting. So was Crispin. And Aunt Lucrece. And Phaon. The painting was what was real. And it kept changing. Whole sections would disappear and if they came back, they were different than they had been." She stared at him. "While you were

140

painting the maze, you changed part of it, didn't you? You painted out a section and did something else with it."

"Yes," he allowed, his face more reserved than before. "I did. The light was changing and I wanted to make the most of it." He gave her a long, thoughtful stare in silence. Then he made up his mind. "I suspect you have some notion of what you want done, based upon what happened yesterday."

"And the day before, yes." Again she was talking too fast, but she had to get the words out before her courage failed her. "Yes, sir, I do. I think you could help me a lot if you were willing to take out the picture with the moat in it, and work on it. I think that would bring it back in the right place, and—"

"I worked on that in the early afternoon. The light isn't the same at this hour of the morning."

"I can see that." She felt her hands knot in anger.

He shrugged. "Then I am helpless."

Quite suddenly anger claimed her. "Helpless? *Helpless?* You're the one who makes all the changes. You're about as helpless as . . . as an Uzi." Let him try to figure out what that means, she thought in triumph. Maybe it would jar him into thinking about what she was telling him. "You change things and people on whim, you make whole buildings go away. You put new things in their place. You change the way these fields are planted. You put a little white paint over something and it's gone into the mist. You aren't helpless. We are."

He gave her another blunt stare. "I am trying to finish this study before the sun is too high overhead."

Geena realized she ought to make a stab at apologizing for her outburst but the words would not come. "So you're going to leave us all stranded? Or are you going to paint me into someone else, so I won't bother you again?" Fear made her voice shake.

"It is a tempting thought," he said. "But if I have truly made such arbitrary transformations, I suppose I should

141

give you the opportunity to try to prove your point. When I have done here I would be willing to try your suggestion."

She looked at him in shock. "Really?" Her voice had shot up almost an octave. "You'll help me?"

"That remains to be seen," he answered. "But you have convinced me that it is possible to achieve this thing you have in mind. So I will bring the canvas and meet with you by the castle as soon as I have dined." He made a motion as if to shoo away a fly or other pesky insect. "Now, if you will, at least, leave me to my work? If I am to do the thing you wish of me, I would like to make some progress this morning."

She nodded quickly. "Sure. I'll get out of here right away." She glanced over her shoulders. Still no crows. "Where should I go until then?" she asked.

"I don't care, so long as it is not a place where you will distract me." He was busy spreading colors on his pallet. "I cannot concentrate with you prattling beside me."

At another time she might have protested his using such language usually reserved for babies, but not now. She stepped back. "Oh, thank you, Mr. Monet. Thank you."

He wagged his brush at her in answer.

As she hurried away in the general direction of the castle, she hoped he would let the building remain where it was long enough for her to retrieve her jeans. But more than that, she hoped she could find the place on the bank of the moat where she had tied the boat. If Monet would not paint it in, she would still not be able to get back, unless she swam across.

20

On her walk to the castle, Geena thought about what she would tell everyone when she got home. It made her feel she was getting somewhere and it helped her to forget the blister on her foot. She considered the facts. She'd been gone for two days. She'd have to give an explanation for her absence, and it would have to make sense. She would probably have to say something to the cops, too. That was the tricky part, because the cops would never understand about what had happened to her if she told them the whole truth. They'd probably think she was nuts, or had done something terrible. What could she tell them that would keep her from getting into trouble? She concentrated on thinking up a plausible story.

She would say that she met a friend at the museum, who was there with his aunt. They invited her to come with them to the aunt's house out in the country, and Geena had thought it was a great opportunity, especially since the storm going on had canceled soccer for the next few days. So far, so good. And it was close enough to the truth that she shouldn't have trouble remembering it. Once at the country house, they were going to phone, but it was out of order. The cops would probably want to know why it was out of order. Geena thought this over. It had to be because of the heavy rains, and there had been reports of some flooding. The flood did something to the power. Yes. That was it. And it was why she was stranded there until the flooding stopped.

As she entered the kitchen door, Geena was grinning. She had an answer that might not be perfect but it made enough sense and it would hold up.

143

"There you are," said Crispin in a combination of relief and aggravation. Today he looked like what he was, a French schoolboy in a school jacket and grey slacks. Geena decided she liked him the other way better, in his semi-medieval finery. Did this mean he was now Albert, or was he still Crispin? "I was afraid you were still in the maze when it vanished."

"I was," she said as she went into the kitchen. This, she noticed, had not changed much, though there was a gaslight lantern hanging over the central chopping table that had not been there before. Benoite was nowhere in sight, and Geena decided she would not ask about her.

"Then how did you get out of it?" he asked, his voice sharpening. "Is there a way out? Did you find it?" He followed after her, dogging her progress. "And your dress is different."

"So are your clothes," she said, looking toward the pantry where her jeans ought to be. "I'm going to change, in any case."

He stopped, astounded. "You mean the ghost—"

She halted long enough to shake her head. "No, silly. I mean I'm going to put my own things back on. Monet is going to try to send me home."

"Who is that?" asked Crispin, very much bewildered. "And please, do not wear those terrible trousers of yours. What if anyone should see you?" This plea was so heartfelt that Geena was almost convinced she should keep the dress on. But how could she account for it back home? Her family might accept her story, but not if she showed up in a costume out of a swashbuckling movie.

She ducked into the room and looked for the rack as she tried to work the laces up her back, recalling belatedly how difficult it had been to fasten them, two outfits ago. "Can you help me get out of this?" she asked Crispin, who was standing in the door, trying not to pry.

"Certainly not. It would be most improper." He blushed

144

as if the very idea of putting his hand to the laces was unthinkable.

"I'm not going to bite," she said, trying to make him realize she just wanted to get changed. "Come on," she urged. "I can't do this by myself without tearing the dress." And it hurt her injured hands to try to unfasten the knots.

Awkwardly he came up to her, standing behind her with his eyes averted as he fumbled with the laces. "I shouldn't be doing this."

"But it's nice you are," said Geena as she felt the knots loosen and give way. "Great. I can take it from here." She was amazed at the energy she had now, as if everything that had exhausted her was lifting from her shoulders. She heard Crispin leave the room hastily as she bent over to wriggle her way out of the dress, letting it drop into a shimmering puddle. Looking at it, she had to admit the fabric was beautiful, but she couldn't understand why anyone would want to dress that way all the time.

Shivering in her underwear, she looked around for her jeans and shirt, and found them at last, stuck on a shelf with a number of scarves and hats. She scrambled into them gratefully, and welcomed them like old friends. *Zippers,* she thought as she closed the front of her jeans. *I've never really appreciated zippers.* Buttons were good, a lot better than laces, but zippers were terrific. Then she remembered her green sweater tied to the tree where she had left the boat. It was probably too much to hope that it would still be there.

As she went out into the kitchen again, she saw Crispin standing near the stove, a mitt on his hand as he reached for the boiling kettle.

"I'm making chocolate. The milk and the chocolate are already in the mugs. I take it you'll want some." He began to pour without waiting for her answer.

"Thanks," she said, realizing he was offering her a truce. "Tell me," she said, watching him set the kettle back on the stove. "Is your name really Albert?"

145

If the question shocked him, he did not show it. "Sometimes. When I am here with my aunt, I am Crispin. It is part of my name." He looked at her, shook his head once at the way she was dressed. "Why do you ask?"

"Just curious," said Geena. "Is there a Phaon in your name, too?"

"No," he replied at once. "What gave you such an idea? Phaon!" he scoffed.

"Someone I met," she said, meaning both the faun and the painter. "And Lucrece really is your aunt?"

"Yes, of course," he said with asperity. "I would not be visiting her without supervision if we were not related." He said this as if it were obvious to both of them. "You can't tell me that girls at your Washington High are such hoydens that they visit those who are not their relatives without supervision. Not even the Americans are so careless."

"Don't you visit the houses of your school friends without . . . supervision?" she asked, certain he was being overly correct. "I bet you do."

"Naturally. But I am almost a man. It's different for men, you know." With that he pushed one of the mugs in her direction. "It's hot."

It was tempting to throw the chocolate at him, the way girls did in movies when a boy said something that insulted them. But this wouldn't be such a good idea with Crispin. And probably not with anyone else. "I'll be careful," she said, and sipped the chocolate.

Crispin gave her a look that was eloquently doubtful.

The chocolate was hotter than she thought. Her lip felt blistered and a large amount of chocolate splashed on her shirt as she quickly put the mug down. She touched her lip gingerly, tears stinging her eyes. She swore.

"Another Washington High skill, I presume?" he said as he came to help her. "You've ruined your shirt."

"It'll wash out," she said, paying no attention to the damage done.

"Not this. It will leave a stain. Chocolate always does," he informed her with the conviction of experience.

"If you say so," she responded, satisfied that the blister on her foot was the only real damage she had sustained so far, that, and the scrapes on her hands.

"I can produce shirts to prove it," he said. "Take that off. I'll bring you one of my athletic jerseys. There are three or four clean ones in my room." With that, he bolted from the kitchen, leaving Geena to examine the stain, only to return quickly with a dark green-and-grey-striped rugby shirt in his hand. "Here. You can have this. I won't need it. I have others." He thrust it at her and turned his back so that she could change.

The jersey was large on her, which Geena thought was great. The fabric was heavy and soft, of a texture she had never encountered before. As she wadded her own shirt into a ball, she said, "Thanks, Crispin. I really appreciate it."

He mumbled something, still facing away from her, then swung around to confront her. "You're really going to try to leave, aren't you?"

"Yes. I really am," she said, and added, "I'll miss you." It surprised her to realize how much she meant it.

He stared at her. "I wish you didn't have to. I know you do, but . . . it would be pleasant to have you here." His cheeks were scarlet.

Geena chuckled, though part of her felt like crying. "That wasn't what you were saying while we were in the castle mist."

"I know," he admitted at once. "That was my aggravation talking. I should never have been so . . . curt with you. You were so brave. In fact," he said, swallowing hard in preparation, "I think you are quite the bravest girl I've ever met."

Now it was really hard not to cry. Geena made herself smile at him, though all the muscles in her face

147

and neck hurt with the effort. "You're no wimp yourself, Crispin."

He looked puzzled—he didn't understand *wimp*—but he accepted it as a compliment. "That's kind." Then he leaned forward abruptly, kissed her cheeks, then stepped back. "I have things to do," he said, and fled.

"Good-bye," Geena said to his retreating figure. She looked around the kitchen, wondering where to leave her stained shirt. Finally she draped it over one of the towel pegs, paused to wipe her eyes—she told herself it was her blister that made her cry, but she knew that wasn't so—before going out through the kitchen door into the garden and across the orchard to the edge of the stream to find Monet.

When she reached the place she expected to find him, she felt a moment of panic because he was nowhere in sight. She looked toward the castle, and saw that it was in the place she remembered seeing it for the first time, though it had had three towers then. She glanced down toward the bank in the hope of finding the boat tied up there, but there was no sign of it. Suppressing a quiver of alarm, she went back to the place she and Monet were supposed to meet.

Maybe, she thought, he won't come. Or maybe he had changed the place so she wouldn't be able to reach him. Maybe he had forgotten. She had read that it wasn't uncommon for painters to get lost in their work. Maybe he was just as lost as she. And if he was, did that mean she was stuck here forever?

The painter arrived shortly after midday, still in his smock, and with his hat squarely on his head. His portfolio and easel were tucked firmly under his arm and his paint box clutched in his other hand; he handled them with the ease of long practice. "There you are!" he exclaimed as he approached Geena. "I was beginning to think you were a figment of my imagination." He regarded her critically.

"What dreadful clothes. Where did you get such improper garments?"

"I wear them to school," she said, not wanting to have the clothes argument all over again.

He made a huffing noise but paid no more attention to her as he set up his easel and dragged a partially completed painting from his portfolio. "I do not like having to do these things in haste. Here," he went on, handing her another sketchbook. "Look through it until you find something that looks familiar." He had set up his box of supplies and was preparing his colors. "I will be ready shortly."

Geena became nervous as she flipped through the pages of sketches. What if none of them were like the painting? Would she be able to get back? She examined each page with hope. Finally, toward the back of the book, she came upon a sketch that looked more like the painting she had entered than any of the others. She studied it carefully, turning the book upside down in order to see if the balance was like the painting. It was hard to be certain about the sketch because it was in black and white and the painting was in glorious, shimmering color, but it had something of the look. She turned the rest of the pages, in case he had another study more like the painting. No luck.

She handed Monet the sketchbook open to the page she had chosen. "It's something like this. The colors make a big difference, but this is pretty much the layout."

He took it from her and nodded. "Very well. I will work on the moat."

She watched as he began to put color on the canvas. It was mesmerizing, seeing the flat white turn into glowing depth. "Oh," she said, as the idea returned. "I'll need a boat. Something I can pole across the moat."

He nodded again, caught up in his work. "Down by the bank," he said gruffly. A smear of brown became a blunt prow. A moment later the boat was in the painting.

Geena glanced down to the stream and saw a boat tied to a tree there. She sighed with relief.

More color filled the canvas, bringing the brightness of the day to it. Monet's face was set with intensity as he wielded his brush. Without taking his eyes from his work, he said, "You had better leave now. The light will change soon, and from what you have said, you must go with the light."

She would not have put it that way, but she took his point. "Yes." Then, as her pulse leaped with excitement, she said, "Thanks. For everything," as she started down the slope to the boat.

The rope holding it to a tree stump was easily untied. She felt the boat tugged by the current as she prepared to climb in. It rocked as she stepped into it and she had to use the pole to steady herself. She fixed her position, took hold of the pole, and pushed off into the moat and the expanse of water lilies. The sun off the moat all but blinded her as she pushed toward the other side. The prow hit an invisible barrier. Geena lurched forward.

She found herself on a marble floor facing an arched doorway. The lights were low and there was no one about, though the room was sunny enough. Then she remembered the museum didn't open until two in the afternoon, and right now it was about one-thirty. Looking down, she saw she was still wearing Crispin's jersey. The whole adventure was real! She hadn't dozed off and dreamed everything. She patted her pockets, hoping to find a couple of quarters for a phone call. Nothing. Her wallet had vanished at the tower. She'd have to walk home, too, because she'd lost her bus tokens. Strangely enough, none of this seemed to matter, not the scrape on her hands—still there—and the blister on her foot.

She swung around and saw the *Water Lilies* hanging on the wall behind her. Impulsively, she got up and went to check the card next to it, for the year it was painted.

1898, it read.

"That can't be right," she murmured. "It was 1893. . . ."

Then she smiled, and her satisfaction went all the way to her feet, and with a happy sense of accomplishment, she sat down on the bench facing the painting and waited for the museum to open so she could finish her journey home.